The Banished
A Swabian Historical Tale
Vol. 2

By

Wilhelm Hauff

The Banished
A Swabian Historical Tale
Vol. 2
by Wilhelm Hauff

ISBN: 978-93-60468-52-1
Published by

DOUBLE 9 BOOKS

2/13-B, Ansari Road
Daryaganj, New Delhi – 110002
info@double9books.com
www.double9books.com
Tel. 011-40042856

ABOUT THE AUTHOR

The Württemberger artist and author Wilhelm Hauff was born on November 29, 1802, and died on November 18, 1827. Hauff was born in Stuttgart. His father, August Friedrich Hauff, was a secretary in the Württemberg ministry of foreign affairs, and his mother, Hedwig Wilhelmine Elsaesser Hauff, was a teacher. He was the second of four kids. When Hauff was seven years old, he lost his father. He learned most of what he knew in the library of his maternal grandfather in Tübingen, where his mother had moved after her husband died. From 1818 to 1820, he went to school at the University of Tübingen. In 1818, he was sent to the Klosterschule at Blaubeuren. He studied philosophy and theology at the Tübinger Stift for four years and was done. After graduating from college, Hauff worked as a tutor for the children of General Baron Ernst Eugen von Hugel (1774–1849), who was the minister of war for Württemberg. It was for these children that he wrote his Marchen (fairy tales), which were later collected in the Marchen Almanach auf das Jahr 1826 (Fairytale Almanac of 1826, also known as Tales of the Caravan, Inn, and Palace in the US).

CONTENTS

CHAPTER XV

Art thou troubled, maiden? Tell me what,--

Thou speak'st of matters which beseem thee not.

Schiller.

Barbelle went up stairs to her mother, who was still occupied in adorning her little plump person, to appear before her guest in proper attire. They then descended together to the kitchen on the ground floor, which adjoined the apartment of Albert. The attention of the good matron was more excited by getting a peep at him through a small window looking into his room, than in preparing a mess of oatmeal porridge for his mid-day meal. Barbelle was also determined to satisfy her curiosity in like manner, and standing upon tiptoes, looked over her mother's shoulders.

She beheld the young man with wondering eyes, and her heart beat violently for the first time in seventeen years at the sight of his fine figure. She had been often moved to tears as he lay on the bed of sickness, insensible, almost lifeless; deeply affected at the pallid appearance of his fine manly features struggling with death, as she imagined, she had watched him with the tender anxiety of a pious mind; but now she felt he was quite a different object to behold. His eye was reanimated by a beautiful expression, and it struck Barbelle, young though she was, that she had never seen the like before. His hair fell no longer in wild disorder over his forehead; it now hung down his neck arranged with care and combed into neat curls. The colour had returned to his cheeks, and his lips were as fresh as cherries on the festivals of Peter and Paul; and how well did his embroidered silk jacket become him, and the broad white collar which he had put on over his dress! But the little girl could not comprehend why he was so much occupied with a certain white and blue silk scarf; she even thought that he pressed it to his heart and raised it to his lips, full of the devotion which is paid to some esteemed relic.

The elderly matron had, in the meantime, satisfied her curiosity in the examination of her guest, and returned to her culinary occupations. "The gentleman looks like a prince," she said, as she gave the mess of oatmeal porridge a stir, "what a jacket he has! no Stuttgardt beau can boast of a finer one. But what is he always doing with that band he holds in his hand? He never ceases to look at it. Perhaps there is a spot of blood on it which he cannot get out?"

"No, that's not it!" said Barbelle, who could now look into the room with greater ease. "But do you know, mother, what I think? he looks at it with such ardent eyes, that it must certainly be something from his love."

The matron could scarcely help smiling at the supposition of her child, but she soon recover her dignity, and replied, "Ah, what do you know about love! Such a child as you must not think of the like. Get away from the window, and fetch me a napkin. The gentleman has been accustomed to good living, so I must put more melted butter in the porridge." Barbelle left the window rather in a pet. She knew that she dare not disobey her mother, but nevertheless thought that she was in the present instance decidedly in the wrong. For, had she not been in the habit of joining the other girls of the village for a whole year past, when they talked and sang of their loves and favourites? Had not some of her companions, who were only a few weeks older than herself their appropriate sweethearts? and should she alone be debarred from even speaking on the subject,--not even to know anything about it? No, it was too bad of her mother; who now forbad her knowing anything about such affairs, when but a moment before she had not objected to her standing upon tiptoes to look over her shoulder. But, as it often happens that prohibition excites transgression, so Barbelle was determined not to rest satisfied until she had discovered why the young knight regarded his scarf with such enraptured eyes.

The breakfast of the young man was, in the meantime, ready, wanting only a can of wine to complete it; this was also soon provided; for, though the fifer of Hardt was a man of low condition, he was not so poor that his cellar could not produce a bottle or two upon extraordinary occasions. The girl carried the wine and bread, whilst her mother, dressed in her complete Sunday's attire, preceded her daughter into the room, bearing the dish of oatmeal porridge in both hands.

Albert had some difficulty to dispense with the ceremonious respect, which the fifer's wife thought was due to such a distinguished guest. She had once served in the castle of Neuffen, and knew what good manners were, and therefore remained on the threshold of the door, with the smoking hot dish in her hands, until the young man positively ordered her to approach. Her daughter stood blushing behind the round plump matron, and her confused countenance was only occasionally visible to Albert when her mother curtsied very low. She also followed her mother through the number of requisite ceremonies, but felt, perhaps, less embarrassment now than she might have done, had she not had half an hour's previous conversation with their guest.

Barbelle covered the table with a clean cloth, and put the porridge and wine before Albert, who was to sit on the end of the bench under the crucifix, which hung on the wall. She then stuck a curiously carved wooden spoon into it, which, standing unassisted upright, was a proof that the meal was of the best cooking. When the young man had seated himself, the mother and daughter also took their places at the table to partake of the breakfast, but placed themselves at a respectful distance, not forgetting to put the salt between them and their distinguished guest, for such was the custom in the good old times.

During the time that each was occupied with their repast, Albert had sufficient opportunity to make a few passing observations upon his companions. In the appearance of the stately personage who filled the situation of honour in the fifer of Hardt's house, self importance and dignity seemed pre-eminent whilst much kindliness of expression was marked on her features. Had not her better half been a man of determined character, and positive in maintaining the upper hand in the essentials of domestic government, there was something in the bearing of his wife which indicated, that one less bold might easily have been brought under her dominion.

In her daughter's countenance, the combined charms of simple unaffected goodness and innocence beamed forth in all their glory. The purity of her heart, and kindliness of her feelings, were delineated in the delicate lines of her features, and the soft modest expression of her eye bespoke unconsciousness of nature's best gifts. Such was this child of nature, bred and born in the lonely cottage of a restless intriguing peasant; Albert could not behold her without admiration, and owned to himself that, had his heart not been already fully occupied with another, and the distance between the heir to the name of Sturmfeder and the lower born daughter of the fifer of Hardt been immeasurably great, she might have won no insignificant place in it. His eye rested with peculiar pleasure and interest upon her innocent face, and, had not her mother been so much occupied with her porridge, she could not have avoided noticing the blushes of her child, when a stolen look at the young knight by chance met his glance.

"Now that the platter is empty, is the time to gossip," is a true saying; which was put in practice as soon as the table cloth was taken away. Albert had two things particularly at heart. He wished to know for certain, when the fifer of Hardt would return from Lichtenstein, because he only awaited intelligence from Bertha to hasten immediately to her; and, secondly, it was highly necessary for him to learn where the army of the League was at the present moment. To the first question he could not expect any further information, than that which the maiden had already given him, namely, that her father had been absent about six days, but, having promised to be back on the fifth, she now looked for his arrival every hour. The good matron shed tears as she bewailed to her guest how her husband, since the commencement of the war, had been but a few hours at home; how he had always had the reputation of being a restless character; and how people rumoured all sorts of stories about him, which would certainly bring his wife and child into misfortune and trouble by his dangerous mode of life.

Albert tried all means to console her and stop her tears; and so far succeeded, as to enable her to answer his questions respecting the army of the League.

"Ah! sir," she said, "terror and misery are our portion now-a-days! it is just as if a wild huntsman were riding on the clouds, driving over the country with his ghost hounds. They have overrun all the low country, and now the whole force is gone to attack Tübingen."

"So all the fortresses are in their hands?" said Albert, astonished: "Höllenstein, Schorndorf, Göppingen, Teck, Urach--are they all taken?"

"All of them, I believe; a man from Schorndorf told me that the confederates were in Höllenstein, Schorndorf, and Göppingen. But I can tell you for certain about Teck and Urach, as we are only three or four hours' distance from them." She then related that, on the 3rd of April, the League's army advanced to Teck; one part of the infantry was posted before one of the gates of the town, and had a parley with the garrison about surrendering. Every one flocked to the spot to hear the summons, and in the meantime the enemy scaled the other gate. But, in the castle of Urach, there were four hundred ducal infantry, which the citizens would not admit into the town when the enemy advanced. A battle took place between them, in which the soldiers were forced into the market place, where the commander was wounded by a ball, and afterwards run through the body by a halbert; the town then surrendered to the League. "It is no wonder," said the fifer of Hardt's wife, as she concluded her narration, "that they take all the towns and castles; for they have long falconets and bombarding pieces which shoot balls as large as my head, breaking down walls and upsetting towers."

Albert could easily foresee from this information, that the journey from Hardt to Lichtenstein would not be less dangerous, than that which he had already performed over the Alb, for he knew that he would be obliged to pass directly between Urach and Tübingen. But, as the army of the League had been withdrawn from Urach several days back, and the siege of Tübingen necessarily required a large force, he might hope there was no post of any importance occupied by the enemy, in the country through which he would have to travel. He therefore awaited the arrival of his guide with impatience.

The wound on his head was quite healed; though the blow had been severe enough to deprive him of his senses for many days, it was not deep, owing to the feathers of his cap and the thickness of his hair having blunted the sharpness of the cut. He had recovered also of the wounds on his legs and arms, and the only inconvenience he suffered from the result of that unfortunate night, was a debility arising from the loss of blood, and lying so long upon the bed of sickness. But his constitution hourly gained strength, his natural buoyancy of spirit resumed its sway, and his only thought was to proceed onwards to his destination.

He was, however, compelled to summon up all his spirits, to make the tedious hours he was still doomed to pass in his present quarters at all bearable. The daughter of the fifer, perceiving how the prolonged absence of her father distressed him, did her best to beguile the time by amusing him with her cheerful conversation. The delay was nevertheless not without its advantages, for he became acquainted with the character and life of the Swabian peasant. Their manners and dialect were quite new to him. His countrymen, the Franconians, although bordering so near on this part of Würtemberg, were to his mind a race more subtle and crafty,--in many respects less polished,--than these. But the kind-hearted honesty of the Swabians, which their looks, address, and actions bespoke,--their cheerful industry, their cleanliness and order, giving to poverty a respectable, indeed a substantial, appearance; in short, everything he saw induced him to think they possessed more intrinsic good qualities than their shrewder neighbours.

He was very much taken with the unaffected simplicity of the young girl's talk. Her mother might scold as much as she liked, and remind her continually of the high rank of the knight, she was not to be deterred from entertaining him, and she was particularly bent upon not giving up her secret plan to ascertain whether she or her mother were right in their views respecting the white and blue scarf. Upon this subject she had her own thoughts, arising out of the following circumstance:

One night when Albert was very ill, she had remained up late to keep her father company, who was watching by his bed-side. But having fallen asleep over her work, she was aroused, it might have been about ten o'clock, by a noise in the room. She saw a man in earnest conversation with her father, whose features did not escape her notice, although he tried to conceal them under a large cap. She thought she recognised in the stranger a servant of the knight of Lichtenstein, who had often been in the habit of coming in a mysterious way to the fifer of Hardt, upon which occasion she was always obliged to leave the apartment.

Bent upon knowing what this man had to communicate to her father, she feigned to be asleep thinking he would not disturb her. She was right in her conjecture; and heard the stranger speak of a young lady, who was inconsolable, on account of a certain young man. She had commissioned him to go to Hardt to ascertain the truth of the report which had given her great concern, and had determined to acknowledge every thing to her father respecting her acquaintance with the invalid, and in case he returned to her with unsatisfactory intelligence, she would immediately proceed to nurse him herself.

The messenger from Lichtenstein spoke in an under tone, as if afraid of being overheard; and her father, lamenting the case of the lady, represented the state of the patient as being likely soon to be ameliorated, and promised that, when he was decidedly better, he would immediately convey the consoling news to her himself. The stranger then cut off a lock of the sick man's hair, folded it up carefully in a cloth, which he carried under his jacket, and being led out of the room by her father, took his departure.

The many occupations of the following days, had driven the conversation of the stranger from the recollection of the fifer's daughter; but when she witnessed the scene from the kitchen window, it came back in full force to her mind. She knew that the knight of Lichtenstein had a daughter, because her aunt had been her nurse, and now was her attendant. It could be no other than this very lady, who had sent the servant to inquire about the sick man, and intended to come herself to nurse him.

All the stories she had ever heard as she sat at the spinning-wheel on a long winter's evening,--and there were many terrible ones, of king's daughters in love, of gallant knights sick in prison, saved by the hands of noble ladies,--came to her remembrance. She did not exactly know what people of quality thought of love, but she supposed that sensation must be much the same kind of thing, which girls of her village felt, when they surrendered their hearts to handsome young fellows of their own rank in life. With this idea strong in her mind, she thought how painful must be the situation of the noble lady, living in the high and distant castle, not to know whether her treasure were dead or alive, nor to be able to come to him, to see him, and to watch over him.

These reflections brought tears into her eye, generally so animated and cheerful. Her heart was touched at the idea of the narrow escape the lady had run of losing her lover; and supposing her to be the daughter of a noble, rich knight, she necessarily must be very beautiful, her imagination led her to fancy her situation to be doubly inconsolable. But was not the young man to be equally pitied, if not more so? thought she. Her father had surely ere this imparted to the lady the gratifying news of her lover's recovery; whilst he, poor man, had not heard one word from her for many days! Has he not been deprived of his senses during nine whole days; and since their return been left in anxious suspense on her account? These circumstances, therefore, left no doubt upon her mind, of the reason why he cherished the scarf with such tender regard, and convinced her from whose hands it came, at the same time that it satisfied her why he constantly pressed it to his heart and lips. Thinking to give him comfort, she determined to relate to him what had passed on that night, when she overheard the conversation between her father and the stranger.

Whilst Barbelle was occupied at her spinning wheel, Albert remarked that she was not so cheerful as usual, that there was a cast of seriousness on her countenance, which he had never observed before. Her mind appeared occupied with a thought that distressed her; nay, he even perceived a tear in her eye. He was so much struck by the change, as to wish to know the cause of it. "What have you at heart, girl?" he asked, just after her mother had left the room. "What makes you all at once so silent and serious? you even moisten your thread with tears!"

"And can you be gay, sir?" asked Barbelle, and looked at him inquisitively in the face. "I think I saw something once fall from your eye also, which moistened that scarf. I am sure it was given you by your love; and I was just thinking how much I grieved that you were not by her side."

Albert was taken by surprise at this remark of his young friend, and blushed deeply, which satisfied her she had made a better guess about the mysteries of the scarf than her mother had. "You are not far wrong," he answered, smiling; "but I am not uneasy on that account, as I hope to see her again very shortly."

"Ah! what joy there will be at Lichtenstein when that happy event comes to pass," said Barbelle, whose countenance had now resumed its wonted gaiety.

What could be the meaning of this, thought Albert? could her father have made known to her the secret of his love? "In Lichtenstein, did you say? what do you know about me and Lichtenstein?"

"Ah! I rejoice to think of the happiness the noble lady will have when she sees you again. I have heard how miserable she was when you were ill."

"Miserable, did you say?" cried Albert, springing upon his feet, and approaching her; "was she aware of my state? O speak! what do you know of Bertha? Are you acquainted with her? What has your father said of her?"

"My father has not said a single word to me; and I should not have known there was such a person as a lady of Lichtenstein, if my aunt was not her nurse. But you must not be offended at me, sir, if I listened a little; look ye, this is the way I know it." She then related how she became acquainted with the secret; and that her father was probably gone to Lichtenstein to give the lady comforting intelligence of his recovery.

Albert was painfully affected at this news. He had all along cherished the hope that Bertha would have heard of his misfortune and recovery at the same time, and have been spared much anxiety on his account. He well knew how the cruel uncertainty of his being safe from the vigilance of the enemy's patroles, even had his health been restored, would wear upon her spirits; perhaps affect her health also. Truly his own misfortune appeared nothing, when he compared it to the distress of that dear girl. How much had she not gone through in Ulm! how painful the separation from him! and now scarcely had she enjoyed the thought of his having quitted the colours of the League, scarcely had she been able to look forward to a more cheerful futurity, when she was terrified by the news of his being almost mortally wounded. And all this she was obliged to suffer in secret, to conceal it from the looks of her father--without possessing one single soul as a friend, to whose sympathy she could confide the secret of her heart--and from whom she might seek consolation. He now felt more than ever how necessary it became to hasten his departure for Lichtenstein; and his impatience was inflamed into anger, that the fifer of Hardt, otherwise a cautious and clever man, should just at this moment remain so long absent.

The maiden guessed his thoughts: "I plainly see you long to be away-- oh, were but my father here to shew you the way to Lichtenstein! It would be imprudent in you to go alone, for there would be no difficulty in detecting your not being a Würtemberger by your speech. Do you know what? I'll run to meet my father, and hurry him home."

"You go to meet him?" said, Albert touched by the proposal of the good-hearted girl; "do you know whether he be in the neighbourhood? he may be still some distance from home; and it will be dark in an hour."

"And were it so dark, that I should be obliged to grope my way blindfolded to Lichtenstein, I'll wager you could not go faster to your----." Blushing, she cast her eyes down; for although her good heart induced her to proffer her services as a messenger of love, she felt confused when she touched upon the tender subject, which had been made so clear to her this day, and which confirmed her in her former suspicions.

"But if you volunteer to go to Lichtenstein out of regard for me, there is no reason why I should not accompany you, rather than remain behind, to await the arrival of your father. I'll saddle my horse immediately, and ride by your side; you can shew me the way until I am far enough not to mistake the rest of it."

The girl of Hardt scarcely knew which way to look, when Albert made this proposal; and playing with the ends of her long plaits of hair, said, almost in a whisper, "But it will be so soon dark."

"Well, what does that signify? So much the better, because I shall then be able to arrive in Lichtenstein by cock-crow," answered Albert; "you yourself proposed finding the way through the darkness."

"Yes, to be sure, so I could," replied Barbelle, without looking up; "but you are not strong enough yet to undertake the journey; and he who has just risen from a sick bed, must not think of travelling six hours in the night."

"I cannot pay any more attention to that," said Albert; "my wounds are all healed, and I feel as well as ever I was; so get ready, my good girl, we will start immediately; I'll go and saddle my horse." He took the bridle, which hung on a nail on the wall, and went to the door.

"But, sir! hear me, good sir!" cried the girl, in a beseeching tone, after him: "pray do not think of going now. It would not be proper for me to travel alone with you in the dark. The people in Hardt are very censorious, and they would certainly say some ill-natured thing of me if----; better stay till to-morrow morning, when I will willingly go as far as Pfullingen with you."

The young man respected her reasons, and replaced in silence the bridle on the nail. It would certainly have been much more agreeable to him, if the folks of Hardt had been less inclined to think evil of their neighbours; but he could not do otherwise than meet the well-meant scruples of Barbelle in their proper light. He therefore determined to remain the night waiting the arrival of the fifer of Hardt; should he not then come, he would mount his horse by daybreak, and set out for Lichtenstein, under the conduct of his young friend.

CHAPTER XVI

The whispering breezes fan the day,

And gently blow around;

With fragrance passing sweet they play,

And break with dulcet sound.

Now, my poor heart, be not oppress'd by fear,

Those breezes will a better fortune bear.

L. Uhland.

But the fifer of Hardt did not return home that night; and as Albert could no longer restrain his desire to prosecute his journey, he saddled his horse at break of day. His good hostess, after no small struggle, allowed her daughter to accompany him. She was afraid lest such an extraordinary event should furnish conversation, perhaps not to the credit of her child, for many an evening's gossip in the spinning occupations of her neighbours, and therefore reluctantly gave her consent. Upon the consideration, however, of the interest her husband must have taken in the welfare of the young knight, having treated him like a son in concealing him in his house, she thought she could not well refuse him this last piece of service. She accordingly permitted her daughter to go as his guide, upon the sole condition, that she was to proceed a quarter of an hour's distance in advance, and wait for him at a certain milestone.

Albert was affected in taking leave of the kind-hearted matron, who, out of respect for him, had decked herself out in her best Sunday's attire. He had placed a gold ducat in the carved chest, as a mark of gratitude for the attention he had received from her; a considerable present in those days, and a large sum out of the travelling purse of Albert von Sturmfeder. It would appear that the fifer of Hardt never knew a word about this deposit whether it was, that his wife did not find the piece of gold, or that she did not like to inform him of it, fearing lest he might return the present to the donor, and thereby affront him. But so much is certain, that the musician's wife was shortly after seen in church dressed in a new gown, to the astonishment and envy of all the women of the neighbourhood, and her daughter Barbelle wore a beautiful bodice of the finest cloth, trimmed with gold, which had never been seen before, at the next feast, kept in commemoration of the dedication of the church. She was always seen to blush, also, whenever any of her companions felt the texture of the new bodice and congratulated her upon the acquisition of it. Such was the effect which a single piece of gold produced in the village of Hardt, in those good old times!

Albert found his conductor sitting on the appointed milestone. She jumped up as soon as he arrived, and walked with a quick pace beside his horse. The girl appeared much more cheerful than the day before. The fresh air of an April morning had given her cheeks a high colour, and her eyes sparkled with kindness. Her costume was well adapted for a long walk, for her short petticoats did not impede her progress. A basket hung on her arm, as if she were going to market. But neither vegetables nor fruit were contained in it, which was generally the case on such occasions; she only carried a large shawl, as a precaution against April showers. The young man thought to himself, as his companion walked by his side, what a housekeeper she would make for some country swain, who should be fortunate enough to possess her for a wife!

She had inherited much of the vivacity of her father's character. For in the same way that he beguiled the time of his companion on their journey over the Alb, by relating stories and pointing out the principal features of the country, did she draw his attention to the most beautiful points of view of the surrounding vallies and mountains; or imparted to him, unsolicited, the popular anecdotes of castles, or other striking objects.

Choosing the most unfrequented paths, she led her guest only through two or three villages, and rested awhile after every two hours' walk. At last, after having made four such stations, a town was seen about a short half-hour's walk from them; the road parted at the spot of their last halt, and a foot-path to the left conducted to a village. At this point of separation, the girl said: "That is Pfullingen which you see yonder, from whence any child will show you the road to Lichtenstein."

"How! are you going to leave me already?" asked Albert, who was so much charmed with the cheerful conversation of his companion, that the thought of parting from her took him by surprise. "Will you not come at least as far as Pfullingen, where you can rest yourself, and have some refreshment? You don't intend to return home immediately?"

The girl endeavoured to look merry and unconcerned; but she could not conceal an expression about her mouth and eye, which betrayed the pain she felt at parting from her guest, whose presence might have been much dearer to her than she was, perhaps, altogether aware of. "I must leave you here, sir," she said, "much as I would willingly go on with you;

but my mother will have it so; I have a cousin in that village on the hill, where I will remain to-day, and return to Hardt to-morrow. And now may God and the Holy Virgin protect you, and all the Saints take you under their care! Remember me to my father, should you meet him; and," she added with a smile, as she quickly dried a tear, "give my respects to the lady also whom you love."

"Thanks, many thanks, Barbelle," replied Albert, as he took her hand to wish her goodbye; "I can never repay your faithful care of me; but when you get home, look into the carved chest, where you will find something which will, perhaps, provide you with a new bodice or petticoat for Sunday. And when you put it on for the first time, and your true love kisses you, then think of Albert von Sturmfeder."

The young man gave his horse the spur, and trotted across the green plain towards the town. When he had gone about two hundred paces, he turned around to have one more look at his young guide. There she stood on the same spot where he had left her, watching him as he increased his distance from her, with her hands up to her eyes; but whether to guard them from the rays of the sun, as she followed him with her look, or whether to wipe away the tear which stood on the brink of her eyelid as they parted, Albert could not precisely tell.

He was soon at the gate of the town, and, feeling tired and thirsty, inquired where the best inn was? He was shown a small gloomy-looking house, having the sign of a Golden Stag, and a spear and shield, over the door. A little bare-footed boy led his horse to the stable, whilst he was received at the entrance by a young, good-natured looking woman, who conducted him into the room common to all. This was a large dark apartment, around the walls of which were placed heavy oak tables and benches. The number of well-polished cans and jugs, placed in regular order upon shelves, proved that the Stag was much frequented. As it was, there were already many men seated, drinking wine, although it was only just mid-day. They scrutinized the distinguished-looking knight very closely, as he passed their table to the place of honour which was situated at the top of the room, in a kind of bow window of the shape of a lantern, with six glass sides; but their conversation was in no wise interrupted by the appearance of the stranger, for they went on talking of peace and war, battles and sieges, in the way which independent citizens were wont to do, Anno Domini 1519.

The hostess appeared pleased with the bearing of her new guest. She peered at him with a smiling look as she passed him, and when she brought him a can of old Heppacher wine, and set a silver tankard before him for his use, her mouth, which was somewhat large, expressed friendly intentions.

She promised to roast a chicken, and prepare a table for him, if he would wait patiently a little while; in the mean time, she hoped the wine was to his taste. The bow window, in which Albert had taken his seat, was a couple of steps higher than the floor of the room, so that he could easily look down upon and examine the company. Though he was not accustomed to pass much time in inns and drinking rooms, he had a peculiar tact in judging of the characters of men, and from the circumstance of his being more a man of observation than of talk, he now had an opportunity of putting this talent into practice.

The party which was sitting around one of the large oak tables, consisted of ten or twelve men. There did not appear to be much difference in point of circumstances among them, at the first glance; large beards, short hair, round caps, dark jackets, were common to them all; but, upon a closer inspection, three of them were to be particularised from the rest. One, sitting nearest to Albert, was a short, fat, good-humoured looking man; his hair, which fell over his neck, was longer and more carefully combed than his neighbours'; his dark beard appeared also to be the peculiar object of his attention. His cloak of fine black cloth, and a felt hat with a pointed crown and broad brim, which hung on a nail behind him, denoted him to be a man of some consequence, perhaps holding the rank of counsellor. He appeared also to drink a better sort of wine than the rest, for he sipped it with the air of a connoisseur, and when he made a sign that his jug was empty, by putting on the cover, a fashion peculiar to those days, he did it with a certain grace and in more polished manner than the others. He listened to everything that was said with a cunning look, like one who knew more than he would deign to express upon the present occasion. He enjoyed also the privilege of patting the waiting maid on the cheek, or stroking her round plump arm, when she replenished his can.

Another man, who sat at the opposite end of the table, was not less distinguished than his fat neighbour, from the rest of the group; every thing belonging to him was lengthy and gaunt. His face from the forehead to a long pointed chin, measured at least a good span; his fingers, with which he was beating time to a song he hummed to himself, closely resembled the limbs of the spider tribe; and as Albert happened to bend himself, he discovered two long lanky legs, belonging to the same personage, stretched under the table. There was something about the twist of his nose also that expressed self-sufficiency, evidently a prominent feature of his character, for he invariably contradicted the rest of the party, whenever they spoke. His manner altogether was that of one who pretends to unrestrained intimacy with persons of higher rank in life than himself, but who never feels at ease in their society. Albert thought it not likely that he belonged to the town of

Pfullingen, for he occasionally inquired of the hostess after his horse, and forming his opinion upon the whole bearing of this extraordinary looking person, he supposed him to be a travelling doctor, who in those days rode about the country, dispatching people professionally.

The third person who attracted Albert's observation was ill-conditioned, and raggedly clothed; but there was something quick and cunning in his appearance, that distinguished him from the good-humour and tranquillity of his companions, particularly the fat man. He wore a large plaister over one of his eyes, whilst the look of the other was bold and sharp. A large walking stick, with an iron spike at the end, lay beside him, and a well-worn leather back to his coat, upon which he probably carried a basket or box, prompted the idea of his being either a messenger, or more likely a travelling pedlar, one who visits fairs and festivals, bringing wonderful news from distant lands, remedies for women against mad animals, and all sorts of coloured ribands and silks for girls.

These three men led the conversation, which only now and then was interrupted by an expression of astonishment from the rest of the worthy burghers, or by the noise of the covers of their wine cans.

One subject, among others, appeared the principal point of discussion between them, and drew the attention of Albert. They spoke of the undertakings of the League in the low land of Würtemberg. The pedlar with the leather back related the storming of Möckmühl by the League, where Götz von Berlichingen had shut himself up with many brave followers, and where that iron-fisted man was made prisoner.

The counsellor smiled knowingly at this piece of news, and took a long draught of wine; Raw-bones did not permit the leather back man to finish his story, but beating time with renewed force with his long fingers, said, with sepulchral voice, "That's a rank lie, friend! it is impossible, d' ye see; because Berlichingen understands the art of war, and is a determined man; I ought to know that; and besides, he alone, with his iron hand, has in many a battle killed two hundred men as dead as mice; do you suppose then that such a man would allow himself to be taken?"

"With your permission," interrupted the fat gentleman, "you are wrong in what you say, because I know that Götz is, in fact, a prisoner, and is now confined in Heilbron. He did not surrender himself, however; neither was his castle of Möckmühl stormed; but when he was marching out of the gate, the League having promised him and his followers a free retreat, they fell on him, took him prisoner, and killed many of his men. That was not fair, and he has been infamously treated."

"I must beg of you, sir," said the thin man, "not to speak of the League in such terms; I am acquainted with many of the officers, for example, Herr Truchses von Waldburg is my most intimate friend."

The fat man looked big, and appeared as if he wished to make a reply, but, upon second thoughts, washed the words which were upon the tip of his tongue, down his throat with a draught of wine. The other burghers, however, broke out in a murmur of astonishment at the mention of such a high acquaintance, and raised their caps out of respect.

"Well, if you are so well acquainted with the movements of the League, as you pretend to be," said the pedlar, with something of a haughty mien, "you will be able to give us the last intelligence respecting the state of Tübingen."

"It whistles out of its last hole," answered the rawbone man; "I was there but a short time ago, and saw most formidable preparations for the siege."

"Eh!--what?" whispered the inquisitive burghers among themselves, and drew nearer, expecting to hear some important news.

The thin man leaned back on his chair, grasped the handle of his sword with his long fingers, stretched out his legs a yard further, and said, with an air of triumph, "Yes, yes, my friends, it looks very bad there; the surrounding places in the neighbourhood have suffered; all the fruit trees have been cut down, the town and castle furiously bombarded, the former having already surrendered. Forty knights, indeed, still defend the castle; but they cannot hold out their tottering walls much longer!"

"What tottering walls do you talk of?" cried the fat man; "whoever has seen the castle of Tübingen, must not talk of tottering walls. Are there not two deep ditches on the side towards the mountains, which no ladder of the League can scale, and walls twelve feet thick, with high towers, whence the falconets keep up no insignificant fire, I can tell you?"

"Battered down, battered down!" cried the thin man, with such a fearful hollow voice, as made the astonished burghers think they heard the falling of the towers of Tübingen about their ears: "the new tower, which Ulerich lately built, was battered down by Fronsberg, as if it had never stood there."

"But everything is not lost with that," answered the pedlar; "the knights make sallies from the castle, and many a one has found his bed in the Neckar. Old Fronsberg had his hat shot from his head, which makes his ears tingle to this day, I'll be bound."

"There you are wrong again," said the thin man, carelessly; "sallies, indeed! the besiegers have light cavalry enough, who fight like devils; they are Greeks; but whether they come from the Ganges or Epirus, I know not, and are called Stratiots, commanded by George Samares, who does not allow a dog of them to sally out of their holes."1

"He also has been made to bite the grass," replied the pedlar, with a scornful side glance: "the dogs, as you call them, did make a sally, in spite of the Greeks, and made their leader prisoner, and----"

"Samares prisoner?" cried the rawbone man, startled out of his tranquillity; "you are not right again, friend!"

"No?" answered the other, quietly; "I heard the bells toll, as he was buried in the church of Saint George."

The burghers looked attentively at the thin stranger, to notice the impression this news would make on him. His thick eyebrows fell so low that his eyes were scarcely visible; he twisted his long thin mustachios, and striking the table with his bony hand, said: "And if they have cut him and his Greeks into a hundred pieces, the besieged can't help themselves! the castle must fall; and when Tübingen is ours, good night to Würtemburg! Ulerich is out of the country, and my noble friends and benefactors will be the masters."

"How do you know that he will not come back again? and then----" said the cautious fat man, and clapped on the cover of his goblet.

"What! come back again?" cried the other: "the beggar! who says he will come back again? Who dares say it?"

"What does it signify to us?" murmured the guests; "we are peaceable citizens; and it is all the same to us who is lord of the land, provided the taxes are lowered. In a public house a man has a right to say what he pleases."

The thin man appeared satisfied that none of the company dared return an angry answer. He eyed each of them with a searching look, when, assuming a kinder manner, he said, "It was only to put you in mind, that we do not want the Duke any longer as our master that I speak as I do; upon my soul, he is rank poison to me; so I'll sing you a *paternoster*, which a friend wrote upon him, and which pleases me much." The honest burghers, by their looks, did not appear very curious to hear a burlesque song upon their unfortunate Duke. The other, however, having cleared his throat with a good draught, began a few words of a burlesque parody on the Lord's Prayer, in a disagreeable hoarse tone of voice--a vulgar song, apparently familiar to the ears of his audience--for no sooner had he commenced, than the good taste of the burghers manifested itself by a whisper of disapprobation; some shrugging their shoulders, others winking at each other; symptoms sufficiently evident to the thin man, that the burden of his song was not welcome to their ears. He therefore stopt short, looking around for encouragement; but, finding none, he threw himself back in his chair, with a scowl of contempt on his features.

"I know that song well," said the pedlar; "and shame be to him who would offend the ears of honest men with it. With your permission," he added, addressing the company, "I'll give you one I think more to your taste." Encouraged by the rest of the burghers, excepting the thin man, who squinted at him with scorn, he began:

> Mourn, Würtemberg! thy fallen state,
>
> Thy drooping pride, thy luckless fate!
>
> A Quack, whom even dogs despise,
>
> Presumes to make thy fortunes rise.

Noisy applause and laughter, mingled with the hisses of the thin man, interrupted the singer. The burghers reached across the table, shook the pedlar by the hand, praised his song, and begged him to proceed. The raw bone man said not a word, but looked furiously at the company. He knew not whether to envy the applause which the songster received, or to feel offended at the subject of his song. The fat man put on an air of greater wisdom than usual, and joined in approbation with the rest. The leather-backed pedlar was going on, encouraged by his audience:

> Of Nurenberg he, a knife-grinder by trade;
>
> His friend was a weaver, a man of low grade--

when the thin man, upon hearing these words, and not able to contain his indignation, flew into a violent rage, and vociferated: "May the cuckoo stick in your throat, you ragged dog! I know very well who you mean by the weaver,--my best friend, Herr von Fugger. That such a vagabond as you should calumniate him!" expressing his anger by a frightful distortion of his countenance.

But his opponent was in no wise to be daunted, and held his muscular fist before him, saying, "Vagabond yourself, Mr. Calmus, I know who you are; and if you don't keep silence, I'll twist those pot-ladle arms of yours off your half-starved body."

The crest-fallen guest rose immediately, and pronounced his regret to have fallen into such low company; he paid for his wine, and walked out of the room with the strut of a man of quality.

FOOTNOTE TO CHAPTER XVI.:

Footnote 1: The appearance of these Greeks at the siege of Tübingen was an extraordinary event; they were called Stratiots, and were commanded by George Samares, from Corona, in Albania. He was buried in the collegiate church of Tübingen. Crusius says, he was famous for wielding the lance.

CHAPTER XVII

Hope, faith, and confidence are there,

For all that I esteem are near;

And yet suspicion finds its way,

And makes my hopeless mind its prey.

Schiller.

When the offensive man left the room, the guests looked at each other with astonishment; they were in a state of mind similar to that of one who sees a heavy storm arise, and expects it to burst and overwhelm him; when, behold, it produces little more than a flash in the pan. They thanked the man with the leather back for having driven away the odious stranger, and inquired what he knew of him?

"I know him well," he answered; "he is a worthless, idle fellow, a travelling doctor, who sells pills to cure the plague; extracts the worm from dogs, and crops their ears; eases young women of thick necks; and gives the old ones eyewater, which, instead of healing, makes them blind. His proper name is Kahlmaüser, or baldmouse; pretending to be a learned man, he calls himself doctor Calmus. He fastens himself upon the great, and should one of them call him ass, he fawns upon him as his best friend."

"But he cannot be upon good terms with the Duke," remarked the cunning-looking man; "for he abused him in no measured terms."

"Yes, he certainly is not happy with him; and for this reason--the Duke had a beautiful Danish sporting dog, which had run a thorn deep into its foot. It was a great favourite of the Duke, who inquired after an experienced man to cure it; and it so happened that this Kahlmaüser was on the spot, and tendered his services, with a look full of consequence. The wretch was fed every day with the best of food in the castle of Stuttgardt, and the fare was so palatable that he remained more than a quarter of a-year, doctoring the dog's foot. The Duke one day called for both doctor and dog, to know and see what had been done. The quack, it appears, talked a great deal of learned stuff, to which the Duke paid no attention; but, upon examining the wound himself, he found the dog's foot worse than ever. He laid hold of the doctor, tall as he was, led him to the top of the long flight of steps, so contrived that a horse can mount up to the second story, and threw him headlong down. He was half dead when he arrived at the bottom, so you may imagine that since that time, Doctor Calmus does not speak well of the Duke. He is also said to have been a spy between Hutten and Frau Sabina, and only undertook the care of the dog for the purpose of remaining in the castle to carry on intrigues."

"Really! was he in correspondence with Hutten?" said one of the burghers; "if we had but known that, he should not have come off so cheaply, the vagabond doctor; for Hutten's amorous intrigue is the cause of this unhappy war; and it appears that this Kahlmaüser assisted him in it!"

"*De mortuis nil nisi bonum,*--we ought to spare the dead, say the Latins," replied the fat man; "the poor devil has paid his crime dear enough with his life."

"It served him right," cried the other burgher, angrily; "had I been in the Duke's place I would have done the same; every one must protect his domestic rights."

"Do not you ride sometimes hunting with the bailiff?" asked the fat man, with a peculiar crafty smile: "you surely have the best opportunity to assert your rights; you possess a sword, and could easily find an oak tree to hang a corpse upon."

A loud laugh from the burghers of Pfullingen apprised the stranger in the balcony, that the jealous upholder of domestic rights was not so well able to administer justice in his own house. He coloured up, and murmured some unintelligible words as he put his can to his mouth.

The pedlar, however, who, as a stranger, thought it not courteous to join in the laugh, took his part: "Yes, indeed, the Duke was quite in the right, for he had the power of hanging Hutten upon the spot, without giving him a chance of his life in fair honourable fight. Is he not president of the Westphalian chair, and of the secret tribunal, which gives him the power of dispatching villanous fellows without further ceremony? Had he not the best proof of his treachery before his eyes? Have you ever heard a pretty little song upon that subject? I'll sing a couple of verses, if you like:

> "In the forest he turn'd him to Hutten, to know,
>
> What't was on his hand that glittered so?"
> "Lord Duke, it is this little ring you see,
> This ring which my sweet love gave to me."
> "Hey, Hans, by my troth thou art nobly drest,
> A chain of gold, too, lies on thy breast."

"That, too, my true love gave so free,

A pledge that she would remember me."

"And then it goes on:

"Oh! Hutten, away! nor spare the goad,

The Duke's eye rolls with fury wode;

Away, whilst there is yet time to fly,

The scabbard is voided, his sword is on high."

The fat man put on a serious face, and said, "I would not advise you to go on; such songs in public houses, in these times, are dangerous; they cannot serve the Duke's cause at present. The confederates being round about us, some one of them might easily overhear it," he added, as he cast a scrutinizing glance at Albert, "and then Pfullingen might have to pay another hundred ducats contribution."

"God knows, you are in the right," said the pedlar; "it is no longer the case, as it used to be, when one could freely speak his mind, and sing a song over his glass; but now a man must always be on the look out, to see that a partizan of the Duke's does not sit on one side, or a Leaguist on the other; but, in spite of Bavarian or Swabian, I'll sing the last verse:

"There stands an oak in Schönbuch wood,

It shoots aloft and it spreads abroad;

And centuries hence recorded shall be,

That the Duke hang'd Hutten on that very tree."

When he had finished, the conversation among the burghers sunk into a whisper, which made Albert suspect they were making comments upon him. The good-natured hostess also appeared curious to know who she entertained in the balcony. When she had spread a clean table-cloth over the round-table, and placed the repast she had prepared before him, she took her seat on the opposite side, and questioned him, but with respect and deference, whence he came, and whither he was going?

The young man was not inclined to give her positive information as to the real object of his journey. The conversation to which he had listened at the long table, made him cautious in giving an answer to her leading question, for he felt that in times of civil strife, it was not less indiscreet than dangerous to declare, in a place like a public inn, to what party he belonged. Albert's peculiar circumstances at this moment required him to exercise more than ordinary prudence, and he merely said, "that he came from Franconia, and was going further into the country, in the neighbourhood of Zollern." With this general answer to the question, he cut short any other upon the same subject. But being now in the neighbourhood of Lichtenstein, he thought he might be able to learn something of the family from the loquacious landlady of the Golden Stag. Putting a few questions to her respecting the different surrounding castles and their inhabitants, in the hope of gaining his point, she very soon related to him reports which deeply affected his future prospects; for upon the truth or falsehood of them seemed, to his ardent mind, to depend his future happiness or misery.

The hostess, fond of a gossip, in less than a quarter of an hour gave him the history of five or six castles about the country, and among them of Lichtenstein. The young man drew a deep breath at the sound of that name, and pushed away the plate from before him, to devote his whole attention to what she said:

"Well, the owners of Lichtenstein are not poor; on the contrary, they possess fields and woods in plenty, and not an acre of land is mortgaged; rather than do so, the old gentleman would allow his beard to be shaved off, for believe me he prizes it much, and takes a pride in smoothing it down when people speak to him. He is a severe stern man, and what he has once determined upon must be done; as the saying is, should the bow not bend, it must break. He is also one of those who have continued faithful to the Duke, for which the League will make him pay dear."

"How is his----, I mean--you said he had a daughter?"

"No," answered the hostess, whilst her cheerful face became clouded of a sudden, "I certainly said nothing about her, that I am aware of. But he has a daughter, the good old man; and it had been much better for him that he went childless to the grave, rather than depart in sorrow on account of his only child."

Albert could scarcely believe his ears at these words: what reason could the landlady have to throw out this allusion? "What has happened to the young lady?" he asked, whilst he in vain sought to appear indifferent: "you have excited my curiosity; or is it a secret you dare not divulge?"

The woman of the Golden Stag mysteriously looked around on all sides, to see that no one was listening; the burghers were quietly taken up with their own conversation, and paid no attention to them, and there was no one else in the room who could overhear them. "You, I perceive, are a stranger," she said, after her scrutiny; "you are travelling further, and have nothing to do in this neighbourhood, so that I can communicate to you what I would not confide to every one. The lady who lives there on the Lichtenstein rock, is a----, a----yes; what the citizens with us would call, a wicked girl, a----"

"Landlady!" cried Albert.

"Don't speak so loud, worthy sir; the people will notice it. Do you suppose I would venture to say what I do not know to be certain truth? Only think, every night as the clock strikes eleven, she lets her lover into the castle. Is not that wicked enough for a well-bred young lady?"

"Mind what you say! Her lover?"

"Yes, alas! at eleven o'clock in the night, her lover. Is it not a shame, a disgrace! He is a tall man, and comes to the gate enveloped in a grey cloak. She has so well arranged it, that all the servants are out of the way at that hour except the old porter of the gate, who has assisted her in all her wicked tricks from her childhood. When the clock strikes eleven in the village, she always comes herself down into the court, cold as it may be, and brings the keys of the drawbridge, which she beforehand steals from her father's bed; the old sinner, the porter, then opens the lock, lets down the bridge, when the man in the grey cloak hastens to the presence of the young lady."

"And then?" asked Albert, who scarcely had any more breath in his breast, scarcely any more blood in his cheeks,--"and then?"

"Then she brings food, bread and wine: so much is certain, that the nightly lover must have an uncommon appetite, for many nights running he has demolished half a haunch of roebuck, and drank three or four pints of wine; what else they do, I know not; I guess nothing, I say nothing; but I suppose," she added, with an upward look to heaven, "they don't pray."

Albert was angry with himself, after a moment's reflection, for having doubted for an instant the falsehood of this narration, spun from some gossipping head; or, should there be any truth in it, it was impossible that Bertha could act with dishonour to herself. We are told that, though the passion of love in the young men of the good old times was not less ardent than in our days, it bore more the character of idolized respect. It was the custom, in those days, for the lady wooed to think herself not only not upon an equality, but far superior to her suitor.

If we look to the romantic tales and love stories in old chronicles, we shall find many descriptions of enamoured knights allowing themselves to be cut to pieces on the spot, rather than doubt the faith and purity of their mistresses. Judging therefore from this fact, it is not surprising that Albert von Sturmfeder could not bring his mind to think ill of Bertha, and however puzzling these nocturnal visits appeared to him, he clearly perceived it had not been proved that her father was ignorant of the transaction, or that the mysterious man was her lover. He mentioned these doubts to his hostess.

"Really! you suppose that her father is acquainted with it?" said she; "not at all--I know it for a certainty, because old Rosel, the young lady's nurse----"

"Old Rosel said so?" cried Albert, involuntarily: the nurse, being the sister of the fifer of Hardt, was well known to him. If she had really said so, the case was no longer to be doubted, for he knew that she was a pious woman, and devoted to her charge.

"Do you know old Rosel?" she asked, wondering at the warmth with which her guest inquired after that woman.

"I know her? you forget that I come for the first time to-day in your neighbourhood; it was only the name of Rosel which struck me."

Albert parried this question, being desirous the woman should not suspect he was acquainted with the Knight of Lichtenstein or his family.

"Don't they call her so in your country? Rosel means Rosina with us, and the old nurse in Lichtenstein goes by that name. But observe, she is a particular friend of mine, and comes now and then to see me, when I give her a glass of hot sweet wine, which she loves dearly, and out of gratitude tells me all the news. What I have told you comes from her mouth. Old Lichtenstein knows nothing of the nocturnal visits, because he goes to bed regularly at eight o'clock; and his daughter sends her nurse every evening at eight o'clock also to her apartment. It struck the good Rosel, however, a few nights ago, that there must be some mysterious cause for this conduct. She pretended to go to bed,--and only think what happened? Scarcely was everything quiet in the castle, when the young lady, who otherwise never touches a chip of wood, laid heavy logs on the hearth with her own delicate hands, made a fire, cooked and roasted the best way she could, got wine out of the cellar, and bread out of the cupboard, and spread the table in the dining room. She then opened the window and looked out in the cold dark night, when, just as the village clock struck eleven, the drawbridge rattled down on its chains, the nocturnal visitor entered, and went into the dining room with the young lady. Rosel has often listened in vain to hear the conversation between them, but the oak doors are very thick, and she peeped also once through the keyhole, but could only perceive the head of the stranger."

"Well, is he an old man? What does he look like?"

"Old, indeed? what are you thinking about? She does not look like one who would put up with an old lover. Rosel told me he was young and handsome, with a dark beard on his chin and lip, beautiful smooth hair on his head, and looked very kind and gracious."

"May Satan pluck hair for hair out of his beard!" muttered Albert, as he passed his hand over his own chin, which was tolerably smooth. "Woman! are you sure you have really heard all this from old Rosel? Have you not added more than she told you?"

"God forbid that I should calumniate any one! You don't know me, sir knight! Rosel told me every word of it, and she suspects a great deal more, and whispered in my ear things which it does not become a respectable woman to relate to a young man. And only think how very wicked the young lady must be; she has had also another lover, to whom she is unfaithful."

"Another?" asked Albert, to whom the narration appeared to gain more and more the semblance of truth.

"Yes, another; who according to Rosel's account must be a charming nice young man. She was with her young mistress in Tübingen, and there was a Herr von ---- von ----, I believe he was called Sturmfittich; he studied at the University; they became acquainted with each other there; and the old nurse declares such a handsome couple was not to be found in all Swabia. She was over head and ears in love with him, that's true; and was very unhappy when she parted with him in Tübingen; but now her false heart is unfaithful to the poor youth, and Rosel really weeps when she thinks of him; he is handsomer, much handsomer, than her present lover."

The hostess, who had quite forgotten her household duties in her zeal to relate the gossip of the neighbourhood, was now called by the fat man in the drinking room: "Landlady," said he, "how long must I knock here, before I get another can of wine."

"Coming, coming, sir!" she answered, and flew to the bar to satisfy the importunate man, and from thence she went to the cellar, and then to the kitchen, and was all of a sudden so full of business, that her guest in the bow had sufficient time to ponder over all he had just heard. He sat there, his hand supporting his head, looking with fixed eyes into the bottom of his silver tankard; he remained in that position from the afternoon till the evening; night advanced, and still he sat at the round table, dead to all the world about him, giving signs of life only by an occasional deep sigh. The landlady did not know what to make of him. She had placed herself at least a dozen times near him, had tried to speak with him, but he only looked at her with a staring eye, and answered nothing. She at last got very uneasy, for just in the same way had her good husband of blessed memory gazed at her when he died, and left her in possession of the Golden Stag.

She consulted the fat man, and he with the leather back gave his opinion also. The landlady maintained that he must be either over head and ears in love, or that some one must have bewitched him. She strengthened her supposition by a terrible history of a young knight, whom she had seen, and whose whole body became quite stiff from sheer love, which caused his death.

The pedlar was of a different opinion; he thought that some misfortune must have happened to the stranger, a circumstance which often befals those engaged in war, and that, therefore, he was in deep distress. But the fat man, winking, asked, with a countenance full of cunning conjecture, what was the growth and age of the wine the gentleman had been drinking?

"He has had old Heppacher of the year 1480," said the landlady: "it is the best that the Golden Stag furnishes."

"There we have it," said the wise fat man; "I know the Heppacher of the year eighty, and such a young fellow cannot stand it; it has got into his head. Let him alone, with his heavy head upon his hand; I'll bet that before the clock strikes eight he will have slept his wine out, and be as fresh as a fish in water."

The pedlar shook his head and said nothing; but the hostess praised the acknowledged sagacity of the fat man, and thought his supposition the most probable.

It was now nine o'clock; the daily visitors of the drinking room had all left it, and the landlady was also on the point of retiring to rest, as the stranger awoke out of his reverie. He started up, made a few hasty steps about the room, and at last stood before the hostess. His look was clouded and disturbed, and the short time which had elapsed between mid-day and the present moment had so far altered the features of his otherwise kind, open countenance, as to impart to them an expression of deep melancholy.

The kind-hearted woman was grieved at his appearance; and calling to mind the sagacious supposition which the fat man had pronounced as to the cause of his agitation, she proposed cooking a comfortable supper and preparing a bed for him; but her kind offices were altogether unavailing, as he appeared bent upon a rougher pastime for the night.

"When did you say," he inquired with a altering voice, "when did you say the nocturnal guest went to Lichtenstein? and at what hour did he depart?"

"He enters at eleven o'clock, dear sir," she replied; "and at the first cock crow he retires over the drawbridge."

"Order my horse to be saddled immediately, and let me have a guide to Lichtenstein."

"At this hour of night!" cried the landlady, and clasped her hands together in astonishment; "you would not start now: you surely cannot be in earnest."

"Yes, good woman, I am in real earnest; so make haste, for I am in a hurry."

"You have not been so all day long," she replied, "and you now would rush over head and ears into the dark. The fresh air, indeed, may do invalids such as you some good; but don't suppose I'll let your horse out of the stable this night; you might fall off, or a hundred accidents might happen to you, and then it would be said, 'where was the head of the landlady of the Golden Stag, to let people leave her house in such a state, and at such an hour.'"

The young man did not heed her conversation, having relapsed into the same melancholy mood as before; but when she finished, and paused to get an answer, he roused up again, and wondered that she had not yet put his orders into execution.

While she still hesitated to meet his wishes, and saw he was on the point of going himself to look after his steed, she thought that, as her good intentions were unavailable to retain him in her house, it would be more advisable to let him have his own way. "Bring the gentleman's horse out," she called to her servant, "and let Andres get ready immediately, to accompany him part of the way. He is in the right to take some one with him," she said to herself, "who may be of use to him in case of need. How much do you owe me, did you say, sir knight? why, you have had a measure of wine, which makes twelve kreuzers; and the dinner,--as to that it's not worth talking about, for you ate so little; indeed you scarcely looked at my fowl. If you give me two more kreuzers for the feed of your horse, you shall receive the thanks of the poor widow of the Golden Stag."

Having paid his reckoning in the small current money of the times, Albert took his leave of his kind landlady, who though her opinion of him was somewhat changed since he first entered her house, proceeding from an air of mystery about his character which she could not account for, still she could not conceal from herself, when he threw himself into the saddle by the light of a torch, that she had seldom seen a handsomer youth. She therefore impressed upon the lad who accompanied him to be very careful, and keep an especial look out upon the gentleman, "who," she added, "did not appear to be quite right in his head." Having reached the outer gate of Pfullingen, the guide asked his new master where he wished to go? and upon his answer, "to Lichtenstein," took a road to the right, leading to the mountains. Albert rode on in profound silence; he looked not to the right nor to the left, neither at the stars over head nor in the distant horizon; his eye only sought the ground. His mind now was in much the same state as at that moment when a blow from the hand of an enemy laid him senseless on the ground. His thoughts stood still, hope no longer animated him, he had ceased to love and to wish. But at that time, when he sank, exhausted, on nature's cool carpet, his last thoughts were cheered with the endearing recollection of his beloved, and his benumbed lips were still able to pronounce once more her idolized name.

But that light seemed to be extinguished which had hitherto guided his steps. It appeared as if he had but a short distance still to go in the dark, in order to seek his peace of mind in a light different to that he had fondly hoped to find on the Lichtenstein rock. His right hand went occasionally to his sword, as if to assure himself that at least this companion was faithful to him, for he now trusted to it alone, as the important key by which he might open the door that would lead from darkness to light.

The travellers had long since reached the wood; the path became steeper, and the horse with difficulty ascended the hill with his rider, who was, however, unconscious of all surrounding objects. The night air blew cool, and played with the flowing locks of the young man,--he felt not its effects; the moon rose and lighted up the road, which ascended amidst huge masses of rock and tall oaks, under which he passed,--he noticed them not; time flowed on unobserved by him; hour followed hour in rapid succession, unheeded by his troubled mind.

It was past midnight when they arrived at the summit of the highest hill, and having reached the skirts of the wood, they beheld the castle of Lichtenstein before them, situated upon an insulated perpendicular rock, rising as if by magic from the depths of darkness, and separated by a broad chasm from the surrounding country. Its white walls, its indented rocks, glimmered in the moonlight; it seemed as if the castle slumbered in the profound tranquillity of solitude, cut off from the rest of the world.

Albert cast a troubled glance towards it, and sprang from his horse, which he fastened to a tree, and sat down on a stone covered with moss directly opposite the castle. The guide stood waiting for further orders, and asked several times in vain, whether his services were required any longer.

"How long is it to the first crow of cock?" inquired Albert at last.

"Two hours, sir," was the answer of the lad.

He then gave him a handsome reward for his conduct, and made signs to him to depart. The boy hesitated to obey him, as if afraid of leaving the young man in his present state of mind; but, upon his repeating the sign with impatience, he withdrew with a slow step. He looked back once before he regained the wood, and observed his silent master still seated upon the same stone, under an oak, with his hand supporting his head.

CHAPTER XVIII

This hollow path must be his way,

It doth to Küssnacht lead,

So here I will his coming stay,

And here I'll do the deed.

Schiller.

Much has been said and written in all ages upon the folly of jealousy, but since the days of Uriah the world has nevertheless not grown wiser upon the subject.

The news which Albert von Sturmfeder had heard from the hostess of the Golden Stag respecting the nocturnal visits of the stranger to the castle of Lichtenstein, had created a feeling in his breast to which it had hitherto been a perfect stranger, and he did not possess sufficient coolness of blood, to exercise his judgment with calmness and moderation, upon a subject of such vital importance to his future prospects. Though he was of an age in which an open generous disposition places implicit reliance in the honour of others, yet taken by surprise, as his unsuspicious heart now was, in its dearest affections, the consequences were likely to become fatal to his happiness. The anguish attendant upon plighted faith broken, burnt within him; he could scarcely control the feeling of wounded pride, at being made the dupe of misplaced confidence; that calm judgment which teaches us to discriminate between right and wrong forsook his mind, and the truth was veiled from his sight in an atmosphere of gloomy foreboding. The fiendish associates, contempt, rage, and revenge, which, with many others, compose the steps of the ladder of feeling between love and hatred, now assailed him, and rendered even jealousy a secondary passion in his breast.

Brooding over these tormenting sensations, he sat upon the moss-covered stone, insensible to the chill of the night air, and his only thought was, to meet the nocturnal visitor, and demand an explanation.

When the clock struck two in a village beyond the wood, he observed lights moving in the windows of the castle. His heart beat in full expectation; he grasped the hilt of his sword. A few moments after the lights were visible behind the trellis of the gate, and dogs began to bark. Albert sprang upon his feet, and threw his cloak aside. He heard a deep voice very distinctly say, "Good night." The creaking drawbridge was lowered over the abyss which separates the rock of Lichtenstein from the country; the gate opened, when a man, his hat falling deep over his face, and enveloped in a dark cloak, came over the bridge, directly towards the spot where Albert was standing.

When he had arrived at a few paces from him, the young man called out in a threatening tone, "Draw, traitor, and defend your life!" and advanced on him. The man in the cloak stepped back, drawing his sword; in a moment the two blades met.

"You shall not have me alive," cried the other; "at least I'll sell my life dear!" and with these words the stranger attacked him vigorously, proving himself by the rapid and heavy blows which he dealt to be an experienced swordsman, and no despicable opponent. This was not the first time Albert had crossed blades in anger; for at the university of Tübingen he had fought many an honourable duel with success; but now he had found his match. His adversary pushed him hard, and his attack was maintained with so masterly a hand, that Albert was compelled to confine himself solely to his own defence, when, in a last attempt to settle the affair by one powerful thrust, his arm was suddenly seized by a strong hand from behind, and in the same moment his sword was wrested from his grasp. A loud voice, from the person who now held him fast in both his arms, cried, "Run him through, sir; such assassins don't deserve a moment's time to say their paternoster."

"You do it, Hans," said the stranger; "I am not the one to take the life of a defenceless man; run him through with his own sword, and be quick about it."

"Let me rather do it myself, sir," said Albert, with a firm voice; "you have robbed me of my love,--what further need have I of life?"

"What is that I hear?" said the stranger, and approached nearer.

"What voice is that?" said the other stranger, who still kept a firm hold of Albert; "I ought to know its sound." He turned the young man in his arms, and, as if struck by lightning, he let go his hold. "What on earth do I see! we might have made a pretty business of it!--but what unlucky star has brought you to this spot, sir? How could my people think of letting you depart without my knowledge?"

It was the fifer of Hardt who addressed Albert, and now offered him his hand. He was not, however, much inclined to return the friendly salute of a man who but a moment before was going to perform the part of executioner. Burning with fury, he looked at the man in the cloak, and then at the fifer: "Do you mean to say," said he, addressing himself to the latter, "that I ought to have allowed myself to remain a prisoner in your house, for the purpose of not witnessing your traitorous designs? Miserable impostor! And you, sir," turning to the other, "as you value your honour, defend yourself singly, and not fall two upon one. If you wish to know my name, I am Albert von Sturmfeder, come here for the express purpose of measuring swords with you, to uphold my previous claim to the Lady of Lichtenstein, which pretension, perhaps, may not be unknown to you. I demand my sword back again, having been wrenched from my hand by an act of treacherous cowardice, and let each make good his pretensions in honourable fight. With my life alone will I cease to assert my right."

"Albert von Sturmfeder!" replied his opponent in surprise, but in a friendly manner. "It appears you must be labouring under some mistake. Believe me, that, instead of being your enemy I am much interested in you, and have long wished to see you. Accept my friendship, upon the word of honour of a man; and do not imagine I visit the castle with the sinister views you attribute to me."

He stretched out his hand from under his cloak, and offered it to the astonished youth, who hesitated, however, to take it. The skill with which he wielded his sword, and the heavy blows he dealt out, strengthened Albert in his opinion, that his opponent was accustomed to the use of his weapon; and that he was a man of honourable and generous character, seemed satisfactorily proved in the frank and unreserved manner he proffered his hand when he became acquainted with his name. Under these circumstances therefore he could scarcely forbear trusting to his word. Still his mind could not in an instant shake off doubts of being deceived under the specious dealings of the stranger, which made him undecided to accept, without further reserve, the proffered friendship of a man whom but the moment before he had looked upon as his bitterest enemy.

"Who is it that offers me his hand?" demanded Albert; "I have given you my name, it is but just you tell me yours."

The stranger threw his cloak back, and raising his hat, discovered to Albert, by the light of the moon, a noble countenance, with a brilliant sparkling eye, bearing the expression of commanding dignity. "Ask not my name," said he, whilst a ray of sorrow played about his mouth; "that I am a man of honour, is sufficient for you to know. I once, indeed, bore a name which was upon a level with the most honourable in the world; I once wore the golden spurs, and carried the waving plume of feathers in my helmet, and, at the sound of my bugle, could assemble hundreds of my people around me--but now all is lost. One thing alone remains to me," he added, with indescribable dignity, taking the hand of the young man with a firm grasp, "I am a man, and carry a sword,--

'Si fractus illabatur orbis

Impavidam ferient ruinæ.'"

With these words he drew his hat again over his face, and throwing his cloak over his person, withdrew, and was soon lost in the wood.

Albert von Sturmfeder stood in dumb astonishment, resting on his sword. The commanding look of the stranger, his winning benevolent features, his brave and generous conduct, filled his soul with admiration and respect. Revenge, which had agitated his breast before he crossed swords with him, no longer ruffled it, but gave way to the contemplation of the virtues which his opponent had displayed in his unexpected rencontre with one, whose life he might have taken in the just defence of his own person. But what conduced above all to raise this man higher in Albert's estimation, was the frank and honest manner in which he had disavowed any clandestine acquaintance with Bertha, having confirmed it by a gallant defence of his honour, which he seemed as capable of asserting as he did of wielding his weapon. Such was the result of this adventure upon the mind of Albert, that he felt it relieved of a mountain's weight of trouble and anxiety, with which, but a few moments back, it had been oppressed. The malicious reports of the hostess of the Golden Stag, which he had too readily given credit to, now stung him with shame and remorse. He would willingly have risked every thing at that moment to have gained admittance to the castle, and thrown himself at the feet of his beloved, to implore her forgiveness for having given place to a doubt of her faithful attachment.

When we consider the weight and respect which physical qualities carried with them in those times,--how bravery, even in an enemy, was prized and admired,--and that the word of a gallant man was held as sacred as an oath on the altar;--and, if we further recollect how imposing is the effect of a pleasing outward appearance upon a young, generous mind, it is not to be wondered that the change in Albert's feelings was as decided as it was rapid.

"Who is that man?" he asked the fifer, who still stood by him.

"You heard from his own lips that he has no name, and neither do I know what to call him."

"You don't know who he is," replied Albert, "and still you were present when we fought? Away with you; you deceive me."

"Indeed not, sir," answered the fifer: "it is true, God knows! that in these times he has no name. But, if you must know what he is, I can tell you. He has been driven from his castle by the League, and now wanders in banishment: he was once a powerful knight in Swabia."

"Poor man! for this reason he conceals his person? Well might he, indeed, have taken me for an assassin. I recollect his having said he would sell his life dearly."

"Don't be offended, worthy sir," said the countryman, "that I also took you for one of those who are lurking about to take his life; I came therefore to his assistance, and, had I not heard your voice, who knows how much longer you would have breathed? But what brought you hither at this hour of the night? and what mishap threw you into the path of the banished man? Truly, you may think yourself fortunate that he did not cut you in two, for there are few who can stand before his sword. Some one, I suspect, has been playing this cruel game with you."

Albert related to his former guide the news he had heard in the Golden Stag of Pfullingen. He pointed out particularly the evidence of the nurse, the fifer's sister, which gave it an air of so much probability.

"I thought it would come to that," replied the fifer: "Love has played many worse tricks, and I don't know what it might not have done to me in such a case, when I was young. No one is in fault but old Rosel, the gossip! What business had she to make the hostess of the Golden Stag her confidant, who cannot keep a secret for a moment?"

"But there must be some truth in the affair," said Albert, whose former suspicions were again awakened; "for Rosel could never have said it without some foundation."

"Yes, there is indeed much truth in the report. Everything is as true as she has related. The servants are sent to bed, and the old spy also. At eleven o'clock the man appears at the castle,--the drawbridge is let down,--the doors open,--the young lady receives him and leads him into the saloon----"

"Well, don't you see?" cried Albert, impatiently, "if all be as you say, how could that man swear that he had nothing to do with----"

"That he had nothing of any kind to do with the lady, you would say?" answered the fifer, "without hesitation he can swear to that; but there is one essential difference in the story, which that old goose Rosel certainly never knew; namely, that the knight of Lichtenstein always receives his guest in the saloon, and, as soon as his daughter has placed before him the refreshments which she has prepared, she withdraws. The old gentleman remains with the banished man till the first crow of the cock, when, after having well satisfied his hunger and thirst, and warmed his weary limbs at the fire, he leaves the castle in the same way that he entered it."

"Oh, fool that I was not to have thought of all this before! The truth was close at hand, and I pushed it from me! But cursed be the curiosity and slanderous spirit of those women, who always fancy they can divine something extraordinary in the most trifling circumstance, and whose greatest charm consists in conjecturing improbabilities. But tell me," said Albert, after a moment's thought, "it strikes me very odd, that this banished man should visit the castle every night exactly as the clock strikes eleven-- in what inhospitable neighbourhood does he reside, which obliges him to seek subsistence here at that unseasonable hour? Now, mind, I am not to be trifled with!"

The eye of the fifer rested upon Albert with an expression almost amounting to disdain: "Such gentlemen as you," he answered, "certainly know little of the pain of banishment; you never experienced the horror of being obliged to conceal yourself from the hand of the assassin, shivering in damp caves, living in inhospitable caverns, among the society of owls, deprived of a warm meal and a cheering glass! But come with me, if you have an inclination,--the day does not break yet, and you cannot go to Lichtenstein by night,--and I will lead you to the habitation of the banished knight. You will not ask me again why he visits the castle at midnight."

The appearance of the stranger had excited Albert's curiosity to such a degree, that he willingly accepted the offer of the fifer of Hardt, more particularly as he then would have the best opportunity of finding out the truth or falsehood of his assertions. His guide took the bridle of his horse, and led him down a narrow pathway in the wood. Albert followed, after he had taken a farewell look at the windows of Lichtenstein. They moved on in silence, which the young man made no attempt to break, his thoughts being wholly taken up with the person whom he was about to visit, and the strange occurrence which had just taken place. He recollected to have heard somewhere or other that many staunch partisans of the Duke had been driven from their possessions by the fury of the League, and he thought that it must have been in the inn at Pfullingen, where mention had been made of a knight of the name of Maxx Stumpf von Schweinsberg, whom the confederates were in search of. The bravery and extraordinary strength of this man was the common talk of all Swabia and Franconia; and when Albert recalled to his mind the powerful figure, the commanding countenance of his late heroic opponent, he thought it could not possibly be any other than this knight, one of Duke Ulerich's most faithful followers. The idea of having had an affair with such a man, and to have measured swords with him in fair fight, was particularly flattering to the *amour propre* of the young man, although the result had been left undecided.

So thought Albert von Sturmfeder on that night. And after a lapse of many years, when his noble antagonist had been long reinstated in his rights, and by sound of bugle could as formerly assemble his followers in hundreds, he reckoned it among his best feat of arms to have stood his ground before the brave and powerful stranger.

They were now arrived at a small open meadow in the wood, which terminated in a thick hedge of thorns and briars. The fifer having secured the horse to a tree off the path, made a gap through the entangled branches, and gave a sign to Albert to follow. It was not without difficulty and some danger that he obeyed his leader's directions, who in many places was obliged to assist him with his hand, as they proceeded down a narrow footpath into a deep ravine. When they had descended about eighty feet they came to even ground again, where the young man expected to find the dwelling of the banished man; but he was disappointed. His companion then went to a tree of great circumference, and which was hollow from age, and brought forth two large torches of pine wood, and striking fire by means of a steel and flint, and a small bit of sulphur, ignited them.

Albert observed, by the brilliant light of the torches, that they stood before a large opening which nature had formed in the wall of the rock. This must be, he thought, the entrance to the habitation of the stranger, who, as the fifer had expressed himself, had his lodgings among owls. The man of Hardt took one of the torches, and giving the other to his companion, said, "The path is dark, and here and there difficult to trace." With this warning he went on in front, leading through the dark entrance.

Albert, whose imagination was on the stretch, had expected to be introduced to a low cavern, short and narrow, like the dwelling of wild beasts, such as he had seen about the forests of his own country; but what was his astonishment, when he entered an immense natural cavern, resembling the lofty halls of a subterranean palace! He had heard in his boyhood, from a man-servant whose great-grandfather had been prisoner in Palestine, a story, which had been handed down from generation to generation in his family, of a boy who had been enticed by the arts of a wicked magician into a palace under ground, which surpassed everything in magnificence he had ever seen above it, and displayed to his view whatever the bold imagination of the east could fancy of splendour. Golden pillars surmounted by crystal capitals, arched cupolas studded with emeralds and sapphires, walls of diamonds dazzling the eye by their numerous refracting rays, were united in this subterranean habitation of the genii. This story, which had made a deep impression on his youthful imagination, now came to his recollection, and appeared to be realised in what he saw before him. He stopped every moment in fresh surprise, and holding the torch high up, viewed in amazement and wonder the lofty and majestic vaulted arches which continued the whole length of the cavern, sparkling and glittering like thousands of crystals and diamonds. But his astonishment was still more excited when his leader, turning to the left, conducted him into a spacious grotto, which fancy might figure to itself the magnificent saloon of the subterranean palace.

The fifer could not help remarking the powerful impression which this wonder of nature made on the mind of the young man. He took his torch from him, and mounting a high jutting rock, illumined more effectually the greatest part of the grotto.

Brilliant white rocks composed its walls. The bold arched cupola, formed of innumerable stalactites, from the ends of which hung millions of small drops of water, reflected the light in all the colours of the rainbow. The surrounding rocks were thrown together in such happy confusion, as to give the imagination full scope to fancy it could discover in their grotesque shapes, here a chapel, having its high altarpiece ornamented with flowing drapery; there its corresponding pulpit of rich gothic architecture. An organ even was not wanting to complete the idea of a subterranean church, and the changing shadows thrown on the walls by the light of the torches, resembled the solemn figures of martyrs and holy men placed in niches.

The guide came down again from his position on the rock, after having, as he thought, sufficiently satisfied the curiosity of his companion. "This is called the Nebelhöhle, or the Misty Hollow," said he; "it is little known in the country, excepting to huntsmen and shepherds, and few venture to enter it, as all kinds of fearful stories are abroad of ghosts inhabiting its chambers. I would not advise any one who is not minutely acquainted with its locality to venture down, for there are deep cavities and subterranean waters, whence no one would see the light again, if once entangled amidst their intricacies. There are also secret passages and compartments known only to five individuals now alive."

"But the banished knight," asked Albert, "where is he?"

"Take the torch, and follow me," replied the other, and led the way though a side passage. They had proceeded about twenty paces, when Albert thought he heard the deep tones resembling those of an organ. He drew the attention of his leader to it.

"That is some one singing," the fifer answered, "the voice sounds particularly beautiful and full in these caverns. When two or three men join their voices together, it resembles the full chorus of monks chanting the *Ora*." The music became still plainer; and as they approached the spot, the expressive feeling of a beautiful melody was distinctly heard. They were obliged to bend themselves under the corner of a rock, as they proceeded, when the voice of the songster sounded from above, and broke in repeated echo on the indentations of the wall of rock, until it was lost in the mingled noises of dripping water from the moist stones, and the murmur of a subterranean waterfall.

"That is the place," said the guide; "above there, in the side of the rock, is the habitation of the unhappy man. Hearken to his voice! We'll wait and listen till he has finished, for he never was accustomed to be interrupted, even when he lived above ground." It was with great difficulty that they could catch the following words on account of the great echo and the murmur of falling and rushing water.

> The tow'r from whence my childhood gazed
> Upon the subject fields so fair,
> Now bears a stranger's banner, raised
> Where erst my father's fann'd the air.
>
> To ruin sink my father's halls,
> The portion of my ancestry;
> O'erthrown and unavenged, the walls
> In earth's deep bosom buried lie.
>
> O'er fields, where once in happier tide
> My jocund bugle horn I blew,
> The savage foemen fiercely ride:
> A noble quarry they pursue.
>
> I am their game, the quarry chased;
> The slot-hound follows where he flies,
> Athirst the stag's warm blood to taste,
> Whose antlers[1] are the hunter's prize.
>
> The murderers have bent their bow,
> They ransack forest, hill, and plain;
> Whilst clad in rags I nightly go
> A beggar on my own domain.
>
> Where once I rode in lordly state,
> Whilst greeting vassals bow'd the head;
> I fear to tap the cotter's gate,
> And beg in pity's name for bread.

From my own doors ye thrust me out;
Yet will I knock while knock I can:
All is not lost, if heart be stout:
I bear a sword, I am a man.

I quail not: tho' my heart should break,
I will endure unto the end;
And thus my foes of me shall speak,
"This was a man, and ne'er would bend."

A deep sigh, which followed the conclusion of the song, gave the hearers reason to suppose, that the burden of it had not afforded the unfortunate exile much consolation. A large tear had rolled down the tanned cheek of the man of Hardt as they stood listening; and Albert perceived the inward struggle which this good peasant seemed to contend with in order to compose his mind, and appear before the inhabitant of the cavern with a cheerful countenance. He requested the young man to hold his torch awhile; and clambered up the smooth, slippery rock which led to the grotto whence the sounds they had just heard had issued. Albert supposed he had gone to acquaint the stranger of his arrival, but his guide returned with a strong rope in his hand. He descended half way down the rock again, threw one end of the rope to him, and desiring him to tie the torches on to it, he pulled them up, and placed them in a secure corner in the rock. He then assisted his young master to mount to the spot where he was standing, which he would not have been well able to accomplish alone. Once up there, they were only a few paces from the inhospitable abode of the exile.

We have attempted to describe this remarkable cavern according to its natural formation. Some further observations may be interesting to the reader. The entrance is about 150 feet in circumference; two paths, which form two natural excavations, one of 100 feet long, the other 82, lead from thence, and, taking different directions, meet again in the interior at the distance of about 200 feet. The place where they join forms a grotto, whence, on the right towards the north, higher up in the rock, is another smaller one, the spot to which we have led the reader, to the dwelling of the exile. The whole length of the cavern, from the entrance to the innermost point, is about 577 feet.

FOOTNOTES TO CHAPTER XVIII.:

Footnote 1: Referring, probably, to the arms of Würtemberg.]

CHAPTER XIX

The rugged rocks fantastic forms assume,

Seen in the darkling of the midnight gloom;

And the wild evergreens so dimly bright,

Seem to reflect a kind of lurid light;

This sight so strange may well our knight amaze,

He stops, upon the witchery to gaze.

Wieland.

The spot to which they had arrived in this large cavern, possessed one great advantage, that of being perfectly dry. The ground was covered with rushes and straw; a lamp hung on the side of the rock, which threw sufficient light on the breadth, and a great part of the length, of the grotto. Opposite the entrance sat the stranger upon a large bear skin, and near him stood his sword and a bugle horn; an old hat, and a grey cloak lay on the ground. A jacket of dark brown leather, and trowsers of coarse blue cloth, covered his person; an unseemly costume, but which did not the less set off the powerful shape of his body, and the noble features of his countenance. He was about thirty-four years old, and his face might be called still handsome and pleasing, although the first bloom of youth was worn off by hardship and fatigue, and his beard having grown wild upon his chin, imparted to his look an air of severity. Albert made these fleeting remarks as he stopped at the entrance of the grotto.

"Welcome to my palace, Albert von Sturmfeder," said its inhabitant, whilst he rose from his bear skin, and offering him his hand, begged him to take a seat beside him on a deer skin: "you are heartily welcome," he repeated. "It was no bad thought of our friend the musician, to introduce you into these lower regions, and bring me such agreeable society. Hans, thou faithful soul! thou hast been our major domo and chancellor up to this moment, from henceforth we nominate thee our head-master of the cellar and purveyor-general. Look behind that pillar, and thou'lt find the remains of a bottle of good old wine. Take my beech-wood hunting-cup, the only utensil left us, and fill it up to the brim, to the honour of our worthy guest."

Albert beheld the exiled man in astonishment; though he might have expected to find the energies of his mind unsubdued by the storms of life, still he was prepared to see him brooding over his misfortunes in sullen melancholy, driven by hard fate to seek shelter in these inhospitable regions. What, therefore, was his surprise to find him, on the contrary, cheerful and unconcerned, joking about his situation, just as if he had been merely overtaken by a storm in hunting, and had sought shelter from its violence in the grotto! It was a storm, indeed, more terrible than the fury of the elements which had driven him from the castle of his ancestors, for he was the prey that had taken shelter here from the shots of his murderous huntsmen.

"You look at me and my abode with astonishment, my worthy guest," said the knight: "you, perhaps, expected to hear me bewailing my hard fate--but of what use would that be? As no one can retrieve my misfortune in this moment, I think it the wisest plan to put a bold face upon what I cannot alter. But tell me, am not I as well lodged here as many princes in their palaces? Have you noticed the halls and saloons of this my palace? do not the walls shine like silver, and the vaulted ceilings sparkle as if they were set in pearls and diamonds? and the pillars, do they not glitter with emeralds, rubies, and all sorts of precious stones? But here comes Hans, my purveyor, with the wine. Say, my trusty subject, does that cup contain the whole of our cellar?"

"Your habitation can boast of water, as clear as crystal," answered the fifer, who well understood the cheerful mood of his companion; "the remainder of the wine in the cellar will fill more than three cups, and--as we have another guest to-day--we may indulge a little. Luckily, I brought a jug full of good old Uhlbacker from the castle to-night."

"You have done well," said the exiled knight, whilst a ray of joy flashed from his brilliant eye; "you must not think, Albert von Sturmfeder, that I am a wine-bibber; but good wine is a noble thing, and I love to see the full glass circulate in friendly society. Put the jug down here, worthy master of the cellar, we'll enjoy ourselves, as in the best days of our prosperity. Here's to you, and the former splendour of the house of Sturmfeder!"

Albert thanked the knight, and drank. "I wish I could return the honour, in drinking to your name," he said; "but, as you have already hesitated to give it me, I will not ask it now, sir knight. But here's to you, and may you return victorious to the castles of your fathers, and may your family live and nourish there for ever--huzza!" He pronounced the last word with a loud voice, and just as he set his cup down, he was astonished to hear it repeated by many sounds, which appeared to be voices, coming from the whole length of the grotto: "What is that?" he said, "are not we alone?"

"Those are my vassals,--spirits," answered the knight, smiling; "or, if you prefer it, the echo, which responds to your kind wish. I have often heard," he added, in a more serious tone, "in the days of my prosperity, the success of my house cheered by hundreds of voices; but I have never been more pleased, or more affected, than to have it drank to, by my only guest, and re-echoed among the rocks of these lower regions. Fill the cup, Hans, and drink, and if you can give us a good toast, let's have it."

The fifer of Hardt filled the cup, and glanced a significant look at Albert: "Here's to you, sir, and something which will please you more,--the Lady of Lichtenstein!"

"Hollo, right so, right so! drink, sir, drink!" cried the exile, and laughed so heartily, that the cavern appeared to tremble under it. "Drink out every drop! long may she live, and bloom for you! Well done, Hans! only look how the blood mounts up in the cheeks of our guest; how his eyes sparkle, as if he actually kissed her beautiful lips. You need not be bashful! I also have loved and wooed, and know the state of a light merry heart of four-and-twenty, on such an occasion!"

"Poor man!" said Albert, touched by a sigh of deep feeling which accompanied these last words.--"Have you loved and wooed also? and perhaps been obliged to leave a beloved wife and children to lament and bewail your present misfortunes!" As he said this he felt his cloak pulled from behind, when turning around, the countryman winked to him, as a sign, that it was a subject of all others the most painful to the knight to hear. Albert immediately saw the effect it produced on his features; and regretted having been the cause of giving him pain.

With a look of wild despair, and evidently trying to combat his feeling, he merely said, "Frost in September destroys the beautiful flower which blossoms in May, and we scarcely know how to account for it. My children are left in the hands of rough but faithful nurses, who will, with God's help, take care good of them till their father returns home again." He was so much affected when he spoke these words, that it required no small effort to enable him to resume his good humour. "Hans is witness," he said, after a pause, "how often I have wished to see you, Albert von Sturmfeder; he told me of your being wounded, on that occasion when you were surprised by a party of the League, who probably took you for one of us outcasts; but happily gave you an opportunity to escape."

"Yes, I had a narrow escape," answered Albert. "I almost believe they took me for the Duke, for they were on the look out for him at that time. I would willingly have suffered much greater loss, to be the instrument of saving him."

"Well, that is saying a good deal; are you aware, that the cut which was made at you might have cost you your life?"

"He who takes the field," replied Albert, "must settle all his accounts with the world beforehand. I would certainly prefer falling before the enemy in the field of battle, surrounded by friends and comrades, that I might receive from their hands the last offices of regard and love. But still, to parry the murderer's hand from the Duke, I would have sacrificed my life, at any time, had it been necessary."

The exile regarded the young man with emotion, and pressed his hand. "You appear to take great interest in the Duke," he said; "I should hardly have supposed it; because they say, your heart is with the League."

"As I know you are a partisan of the Duke," answered Albert; "I trust you will excuse me if I speak my mind freely. Well, then, I must tell you, I think the Duke has acted, in many respects, not becoming his high station; for example, he ought not to have meddled in the affair of Hutten in the manner he did, whatever might have been his reasons; and then, the treatment of his wife was excited by violence and an overbearing spirit; and you must admit, that it was rage and revenge, and not a just ground for attack, which moved him to take forcible possession of Reutlingen."

He paused, expecting to hear a remark from the knight, upon what he had just said; but as he remained silent, Albert continued: "Upon these reports I formed the idea of the Duke's character when I joined the ranks of the confederates, among whom he was vilified in still stronger terms; but, on the other hand, he had a warm advocate in the Lady of Lichtenstein, who was better acquainted with his virtues than his enemies, and who you may perhaps have already heard was the principal cause of my quitting their service. I will not, therefore, say more upon the subject further than she opened my eyes to the true state of existing circumstances. In consequence of her information, I gave myself some trouble to penetrate the ulterior views of the League, and found they were directed, not only to the dispossessing him of his dominions and banishing him his country, but, in order to gratify the real object of their views, they grasped at the partition of his sovereignty among themselves. With the impression of the injustice of their intentions strong in my mind, I viewed the Duke's cause in a light totally different to what I had hitherto done. His character was raised still higher in my estimation, when I also learnt, that though urged by the patriotism and love of his people to venture a battle in defence of his rights, he would not risk the blood of his faithful Würtembergers in such a hazardous game. And though possessing the power of extorting money from his subjects to subsidize the

Swiss, he rather preferred exile for the good of his country. These are my reasons for befriending the ill-used Prince."

The knight, whose eyes had been fixed on the ground, now raised them upon Albert, and he seemed overpowered with the kind expressions which he had used towards the Duke. "Truly," he said, "your feelings are pure and generous, my young friend! I know the Duke as well as I do myself, and I may venture to say with you, that he rises superior to his misfortunes, and merits a far better name than report gives of him. Ah! if he had a hundred hearts such as yours, not a rag of the League's ensigns would ever float over the castles of Würtemberg;--could I but persuade you to join his cause! Far be it from me, however, to invite you to share his misery; it is enough that your sword, and an arm such as yours, do not belong to his enemies. May your days be happier than his! may heaven reward your good opinion of an unfortunate man!"

The spirit which breathed throughout the words of the exile, struck many a corresponding chord in the heart of Albert. He was flattered and encouraged to hear his own actions thus acknowledged.

The similarity which appeared to exist between the fate of his unknown friend and the impoverished fortunes of his own house, together with the prompting of the noble desire to espouse the weakest but honest cause in the pending struggle, in preference to taking the side of victorious injustice, were so many irresistible inducements to the manly mind of Albert to stand by the exile in his present deep distress.

Inspired by this feeling, he took his hand, and said, "Let no one henceforth talk to me of the imprudence,--let it not be called folly,-- of sharing the misfortunes of the persecuted! May others partake of the division of the Duke's fine country, and carouse in the spoils of the unhappy man's property,--I feel courage enough to suffer with him in his sufferings; and, when he draws his sword to re-conquer his lost possessions, I will be the first by his side. Take my hand, sir knight, as my pledge: let what may happen, I am the Duke's friend from henceforth, for ever."

A tear of gratitude started in the eye of the exile as he returned the shake of his hand. "You risk much, but you lose nothing by becoming Ulerich's friend. The country, beyond these inhospitable regions, is now in the possession of tyrants and robbers; but here below faithful hearts still beat true to Würtemberg. Forget for a moment that I am a poor knight and an exiled man, and figure me to yourself the Prince of the country, as I am lord of this cavern, with his knight and citizen standing before him. Ah! as long as these three estates hold firm together, be they concealed ever so deep in the lap of the earth, Würtemberg still exists. Fill the cup, Hans, and join your rough hand to ours; we'll seal the alliance in a bumper!"

Hans replenished the jug and filled the cup, "Drink, noble sirs, drink," said he; "you cannot pledge yourselves in a more noble wine than in this Uhlbacher."

The knight having emptied the cup by a long draught, ordered it to be filled again, and presented it to Albert. "Does not this wine," asked Albert, "grow about the castle whence Würtemberg's royal blood sprang? I think the heights about it are called Uhlbacher?"

"You are right," answered the exile; "the hill is generally called the Rothenberg, at the foot of which the vine grows; the castle stands upon its summit, built by Würtemberg's ancestors. Oh! the beautiful vallies of the Neckar, the luxuriant hills of fruit and wine! Gone, gone for ever!" He uttered these words with a voice which bespoke a heart almost broken by suffering and grief; he could scarcely conceal the anguish of his soul, which his inflexible mind had hitherto veiled under the mask of a forced hilarity.

The countryman knelt beside him, took his hand, and to rouse him from a state of painful wandering, in which he was lost for some moments, said, "Be of good cheer, sir; you will return to your country again happier than you left it."

"You will behold the vallies of your home again," said Albert. "When the Duke regains his lost rights, and reoccupies the castles of his ancestors, the vallies of the Neckar, and its richly clothed hills of vineyards, will echo with the rejoicings of his people, and you also will be able to join in the jubilee. Banish gloomy thoughts from your mind, *nunc vino pellite curas*; drink, and let us hope for better times. I pledge you in this Würtemberg wine,--'to the Duke's happy return with his faithful followers!'"

These words seemed to reanimate the sunken spirits of the knight, and like a ray of sunshine shed a smile over his features. "Yes!" he cried, "sweet is the word which sends comfort to the broken-hearted; it is like a drop of cold water to refresh the weary wanderer in the desert. Forget my weakness, my friend; pardon it in a man who otherwise never gives place to grief.

"But if you had ever looked down from the summit of the Rothenberg, shaded by its green woods, into the heart of Würtemberg, and beheld the gentle stream of the Neckar winding its course along its richly cultivated banks; with its fields of high standing corn waving in the breeze; the red roofs of its villages peeping out from a forest of fruit trees, with their industrious inhabitants, consisting of strong men and beautiful women, busily employed in their gardens or dressing their vines on the heights; had you surveyed all this, and with my eyes, and then been compelled to take refuge from the bloodthirsty hands of ruffians in these inhospitable regions, surrounded by the benumbing chill of these walls, outlawed, condemned, banished.--Oh! the thought is terrible! too overwhelming for man's heart to bear!"

Albert, fearful lest the recollection of his past days, and the keen sense of his present situation, might a second time have too powerful an effect upon the mind of the exile, sought by changing the subject of conversation, to divert his mind and calm his thoughts.

"As I suppose you have been often with the Duke," he said, "pray tell me, now that I am his declared friend, what is his disposition? what is his appearance? is it true, as is reported, that he is of a very changeable and capricious temper?"

"No more upon that subject at present, if you please," answered the exile; "you will soon have an opportunity to judge for yourself when you see him. We have already spoken enough upon these matters, but you have said nothing about your own affairs; not a word about the object of your travels, nor of the beautiful lady of Lichtenstein? You are silent and look confused when that delicate subject is mentioned. Do not suppose I wish to be curious when I ask that question; no, it is solely because I think I can be of use to you."

"From what has passed between us this night," replied Albert, "I have nothing to conceal from you; secrecy is no longer necessary. It strikes me, that you must have long known I love Bertha, and that she likewise is faithful to me?"

The exile answered, smiling, "O yes, there was no mistaking the symptoms of her feelings, for when you were mentioned her confused look bespoke the secret of her heart, and the blush which accompanied it was an evident witness of the truth of it. When she named you it was with a peculiar tone of voice, as if the strings of her heart sounded in full accord to that key-note."

"This observation of yours will encourage me to go to Lichtenstein without further delay. It was my original intention, after I had quitted the service of the League, to go direct to my home; but as the Alb is about half way between Franconia and this place, and the desire I had to see my love once more was uppermost in my thoughts, I determined to endeavour to accomplish it. This man Hans conducted me over the Alb; you know the cause which delayed me eight days on my journey. To-morrow, at day-break, I purpose announcing myself at the castle, and I trust I shall now appear before the old knight in a more welcome light than I should otherwise have done, had I not performed my promise to the League of remaining neutral fourteen days, and now joined his colours."

"You may be assured of his welcome," said the knight, "particularly if you go as the friend of the Duke, for he is his faithful and most devoted adherent. But, may be, he would not trust your word, unsupported by some introduction, being, so it is said, rather incredulous, and shy of strangers. You know upon what terms I am with him. He is the kind-hearted Samaritan to me; and when I creep out of my hole at night, he nourishes my body with warm food, and my heart with still warmer consolation for the future. A couple of lines from me will be better received by him than a passport from the Emperor. Take this ring, which he and many others know and respect, and wear it in remembrance of the time we have passed together; it will announce you as a friend of Würtemberg's good cause." With these words, he took a broad gold ring from his finger. A large red stone was set in the middle, upon which was engraved, in the armorial helmet, the three stag horns,1 with the bugle, which Albert recognised as the arms of Würtemberg. Around the ring were the letters, U.D.O.W.A.T. in relievo, the meaning of which he could not comprehend.

"Udowat? what does that name signify?" he asked. "Is it a parole for the followers of the Duke?"

"No, my young friend," said the exile. "The Duke has worn this ring long on his finger; he valued it much; but as I have many other souvenirs from him, I can best spare it, and could not place it in worthier hands. The letters mean, Ulerich, Duke of Würtemberg and Teck."

"I shall value it as long as I live," replied Albert, "as a relic of the unfortunate Prince whose name it bears, and as a pleasing remembrance of you, sir knight, and the night we passed together in this cavern."

"When you come to the drawbridge of Lichtenstein," continued the knight, "deliver a note which I will write, and this ring, to the first servant you see, and desire them to be conveyed to the lord of the castle, when he will certainly receive you as the Duke's own son. But for the lady, you must use your own passport, for my charm does not extend to her: a tender squeeze of the hand, or the mysterious language of the eyes, or perhaps still better, a sweet kiss on her rosy lips, will serve the purpose. But in order to appear before her as she would wish to see you, you need some rest, for if you pass the whole night without sleep, your eyes will be heavy. Therefore follow my example, stretch yourself on the deer skin, and make a pillow of your cloak. And you, worthy major domo, grand chamberlain and purveyor, Hans, faithful companion in misfortune, give this Paladin another glass for his nightcap, it will soften his deer-skin, and enchant this rocky grotto into a bed-room. And then may the god of dreams visit him with his choicest gifts!"

The men drank a good night to each other, and laid themselves to rest, Hans taking up his position as a faithful dog, at the entrance of the rocky chamber. Morpheus soon came with light steps to the aid of the young man, and as he was dropping off to sleep he heard, in a half doze, the exile saying his evening prayer, and, with pious confidence in the Disposer of events, imploring him to shower down his almighty protection on him and his unhappy country.

FOOTNOTES TO CHAPTER XIX.:

Footnote 1: Three stag horns, the two upper ones having four ends and the lower one three, were the ancient arms of Würtemberg.

CHAPTER XX

See that arrowy crag so tapering rise,

From the depths of that valley so sweet;

There Lichtenstein's fort rears her head to the skies,

And smiles on the world at her feet.

Schwab.

When the fifer of Hardt awakened Albert in the morning, the youth was at first puzzled to recollect where he was, and to recognize the objects about him; but he soon came to his senses, and the remembrance of the last evening's occurrences. He returned the hearty shake of the hand with which the exile saluted him, who said, "Although it would give me great pleasure to detain you some few days with me, yet I would rather advise you to proceed at once to Lichtenstein, if you wish to have a hot breakfast. I cannot, alas! prepare such in my cavern, for we never dare make a fire, lest the smoke betray our position."

Albert consented to his proposal, and thanked him for his night's lodging. "I may truly say," he answered, "that I never passed a night more to my satisfaction, than I have done in this place. A deep-felt, though melancholy, charm would seem to hallow the society of friends in such a situation as this, and I would not have exchanged my abode among these rocky walls, for the most splendid apartment of a ducal palace."

"Yes, indeed, secure from persecution, and among friends, when the glass circulates freely, banishment has its charms," replied the exile; "but when I sit here, day after day, in solitude, brooding over my calamities, my heart yearning for liberty, and my eye wearied with the sameness of these subterranean splendours, then it is I drink the full cup of misery. And then again, my ear is deafened with the unceasing monotonous murmur of these waters, dripping drop after drop from the rocks! Jealous of their freedom, my imagination follows their course through the depths below, whence they escape to swell the running stream, whose gentle ripple, with the note of the cheerful lark, would seem to join chorus in the universal praise."

"My poor friend, I pity thee! yes, indeed, this solitary life must be terrible," said Albert.

"Nevertheless," continued the other, raising himself up, "I reckon myself happy to have found this asylum, with the help of a few trusty friends. Rather than fall into the hands of my enemies, to be their sport and laughing-stock, I would descend a hundred fathoms lower, where the vital air scarce sustains life. And before I would surrender my liberty, these hands should dig my way into the heart of the earth, until I reached its centre; there to invoke the curses of heaven upon my oppressors as a just punishment of the wrongs I endure from the persecutions of their revengeful designs."

The exile having worked himself up into a state of fury, Albert involuntarily retreated a pace or two. His figure appeared to gain in height--all the muscles of his body were on the stretch--his cheeks glowed with rage--his eyes shot fire, as if they sought an enemy upon whom to revenge his sufferings; and the loud and violent tone of his voice; echoed among the rocks the maledictions which issued from his mouth.

Albert could not but sympathise with the man in giving vent to his feelings in such a burst of passion; he who was so cruelly persecuted by his enemies, for his faithful attachment to his lord. "I admire your strength of mind," said he to the knight; and, as if a sudden thought had crossed his mind, continued, "will you pardon me for asking you one question, which perhaps you may deem indiscreet; but since you have admitted me to your friendship and confidence, I will venture to do so. Tell me, are you not the celebrated Maxx Stumpf von Schweinsberg?"

There must have been something particularly strange in this question; because the gravity which had shaded the knight's countenance disappeared at once, at the mere mention of this name. He first smiled; but not able to contain himself, broke out into a loud laugh, in which Hans considered himself permitted to join.

Albert was unable to comprehend the meaning of the sudden burst of merriment which his question had occasioned. He felt confused, and looked for an explanation of it, first at one, then at the other; but his embarrassment only excited their merry mood still more.

At length the exile said, "Pardon me, worthy guest, for having violated in an unmannerly way the rights of hospitality; for I ought rather to have bitten off the end of my tongue than have given you cause to suppose I had thought you said anything ridiculous; but how comes it that you take me for Maxx Stumpf? Do you know him?"

"No, I never saw him; but I know him to be a brave knight, whom the League has expelled from his country, on account of his faithful adherence to the Duke, and that they are now endeavouring to apprehend him. Is not yours a similar case?"

"I thank you for comparing me to such a man; but I would not advise
you to fall in his way in the night, upon the same terms as when we met;
for Stumpf, without further to do, would soon have cut you up into slices fit
for cooking. Schweinsberg being a little thick-set fellow, and a head shorter
than me, it was the comparison which made me laugh so irresistibly. He is,
however, an honourable man, and one of the few to be depended upon who
will not desert his master in misfortune."

"So you are not Schweinsberg?" replied Albert; "then I must leave you
without knowing who my friend is."

"Young man!" said the exile, with dignity, "you have found a friend
in me, by your gallant, honourable behaviour; which your open, frank
countenance has confirmed. Let it suffice for you, to have gained this friend;
ask no further questions, one word might perhaps interrupt this confidential
intimacy between us, which is so gratifying to me. Farewell; think on the
banished man without a name, and be assured that, before two days are
over, you shall both hear from me, and know my name."

In spite of his unseemly dress, the whole demeanour of this man
appeared to Albert to be more that of a Prince dismissing a subject from
his presence, than an unfortunate exile, parting from a friend who had
participated in his afflictions.

During the last conversation, the fifer of Hardt had lighted the torches,
and stood waiting at the entrance of the grotto; the knight pressed a salute
on the lips of the young man, and waved him to go. He departed, unable
to account why a man so familiar and friendly in his address, should, at
the same time, inspire him with the idea of being so much his superior in
rank; he had never felt, until this moment, how an individual, devoid of
all the external marks of distinction, exhibiting outward signs of poverty,
rather than the contrary, could possess a personal influence sufficiently
great to subdue vanity and self-love. Occupied with these thoughts, he
retraced his steps through the cavern. The beauties of nature, which had
surprised him and fixed his attention when he first entered it, had lost their
charm to his eye, and his wonder was no longer excited at the grandeur
of the surrounding objects. His mind was exclusively taken up with the
contemplation of a subject more imposing and instructive than these rocks,
however magnificent they might be. The human mind, rising superior to the
frowns of this world, exemplified so well in the character of his unknown
friend, filled him with admiration, and proved to him that the dignity of
man's nature will force its way through the garb of poverty and the suffering
of persecution, and remain unsullied amidst the frowns of fate.

A bright day greeted Albert and the fifer of Hardt, as they issued from the darkness of the cavern into the light of heaven. Albert breathed more freely in the freshness of the morning air, than he had done amidst the damp exhalations which streamed from the galleries and grottos of the subterranean vaults, from which they derive the name of the misty caverns. He found his horse in the same place, fastened to the tree, where he had left him the night before, as fresh and lively as ever; the military weapons attached to the saddle not having suffered from the night dew, which Albert was fearful might have been the case. But Hans had had the precaution to cover the beast with a large coarse cloth, in order to guard against bad weather. The young man arranged his dress as well as he was able, after such a night's lodging, whilst the countryman gave his horse a feed of fresh hay. They then set forward on their journey, and having gone but a few paces, the tolling of a church bell from the valley below saluted their ears, and broke the solemn stillness of the morning. Shortly afterwards, another bell answered, and then three or four more followed, when the number, increasing to at least twelve, spread their melodious tones over the heights and vallies. The young man stopt his horse, surprised at this early chorus of bells: "What means this salutation?" he asked, "is it a signal that there is a fire in the neighbourhood? or may be to-day is a holiday? God knows that, since my illness, I have quite lost all knowledge of time, and can only distinguish Sunday from the other days of the week by the peasant girls being clad in their best dresses and clean aprons."

"That is not an uncommon case with many a military man," replied Hans; "I myself have often been obliged to guess what day it was, when I had other things in my head, which I regret to say I deemed more important than hearing mass. But now it is different," he added, with a serious countenance, and crossed himself, "to-day is Good Friday."

"That reminds me," said the young man, "that this is the first time in my life that I have not celebrated this day as becomes a Christian; it also brings with it many happy hours of my youth to my recollection. My father was then alive; I possessed a tender, good mother, and a dear young sister. We two children always rejoiced upon the anniversary of Good Friday, and, though we did not know exactly what it meant, we remembered that it was only two days from Easter, a season when our mother invariably gave us some token of her affection. *Requiescant in pace!*" he added, turning away to conceal a tear; "they are all three gone."

These last words, which he pronounced in remembrance of his departed parents, the spontaneous effusion of his affectionate heart, did not escape the fifer's observation, who raised his cap in respect to the feelings of his companion. Such had been the restless life of this extraordinary man from his infancy, that he might have been thought to be void of all sense of religion; but since his escape from the hand of the executioner, which he had hinted at in a former conversation with Albert, and professed to have become a better man, serious thoughts at times occupied his mind.

Albert having alluded to his own case of receiving a present from his mother at Easter, the fifer took occasion to say, with a good-natured smile, "that the time was coming, when he hoped he would also be able to perform the same office to his own children." But the young man was offended at this familiarity, and showed symptoms of his displeasure.

"No offence, sir," he replied, and drew his attention to the castle before them. "Do you see the tower peeping out among the trees?" he added: "another short quarter of an hour, and we are there."

"From what I could remark yesterday in the dark," said the young man, "the castle appeared to be erected upon a solitary, steep rock. By heavens! a bold thought, whoever built it; for no one could attempt to scale its walls unless he were in league with the devil, and had the power of flying. It might be bombarded, however, from this spot with heavy artillery."

"Do you think so? I can tell you, that they have four good match-guns in the hall, which would return an answer too sharp to any one who should attempt it. Had you made a careful survey, you must have observed, that the rock is separated from the mountain by a broad deep valley, which surrounds it, so that much damage could not be done to the castle. The only weak side is that nearest the mountain, upon which the drawbridge is placed. Let but an enemy attempt to plant guns there, and he would soon see old Lichtenstein's battery hurl them down in the abyss below, before they had even touched a pane of glass in his windows. But the great difficulty would be to get guns up this declivity, and transport them over these cavities, without exposing men to more danger than that nest is worth."

"You are right," Albert answered; "I should like to know who ever thought of building a castle upon that rock."

"I'll tell you," replied Hans, who was well acquainted with all the legends of his country: "once upon a time there lived a fair lady, who suffered much persecution from her suitors, and did not know how to escape them. She came to this rock, and saw a large eagle with its family perched upon the top of it, secure from all interruption. Having determined to expel the eagle, she built the castle on its nest; and when everything was complete, drew up the drawbridge, and from the summit of the tower proclaimed aloud, 'I henceforth devote myself to God, and forswear the world.' From that day forth no one was able to annoy her;--but we are arrived. Farewell; perhaps I may see you again tonight. I am now going about the country, to endeavour to ascertain what is going on, and will return to the exile in the cavern with what news I can gather as to the state of the Duke's affairs. Don't forget, when you come on the bridge, to send the ring and letter to the lord of the castle; and take care you do not break the seal yourself."

"Don't fear! I thank you for your conduct; salute my kind host of the cavern for me," said Albert; and, pushing his horse forward, in a few minutes stood before the fortress of Lichtenstein.

A guard at the gate demanded his business, and called a servant to deliver the letter and ring to his master. Albert had in the meantime an opportunity to examine minutely the castle and its environs. Having only seen it the night before by the dim light of the moon, and too much occupied with other important subjects to fix his exclusive attention to its structure, he had not been able to imagine even what he now viewed with rapture. A perpendicular isolated rock, like the colossal tower of a cathedral, rising from the valley of the Alb, stood before him in bold independence. Its position impressed him with the idea, that it might have been cleft from the surrounding hills by some violent convulsion of nature, either by an earthquake, or by a deluge in ancient times, which had washed away the softer materials of the earth, leaving the solid mass of rock untouched. Even on the south-west side, where he now stood, the deep ravine which separated the rock from the nearest part of the adjoining country, was too broad for the boldest shamoy to venture a spring across, though not so distant as to baffle the art of man to throw a bridge over. The castle stood on its summit, like the nest of a bird, perched upon the highest branch of an oak, or the pinnacle of a lofty tower. Except the tower, which peered above all, the only apparent habitation was a small fortified apartment surrounded by many round windows. The numerous loop-holes in the lower part of the buildings, and several larger embrasures, out of which peeped the muzzles of guns of the heavy calibre of the time, proved that it was well guarded, and that, spite of its insignificant size, it was no contemptible fortress. The enormous foundation walls and buttresses, which appeared to form part of the rock, and had assumed by age and weather the same yellowish-brown colour of the mass of stone upon which they stood, might well convince the beholder of the solidity of the structure, and its capability to bid defiance to the power of man and the storms of the elements. A beautiful view presented itself before Albert, and he thought how much more extended it must be from the top of the watch-tower.

These observations obtruded themselves upon Albert, as he stood waiting at the outer gate, which was strongly palisadoed towards the ravine, and covered the approach to the bridge. He now heard steps approaching; the gate was thrown open, and the master of the castle appeared himself to receive his guest. It was the same stern elderly man whom he had seen several times in Ulm, whose countenance he could not easily forget; for his dark fiery eye, his pale but noble features, his likeness to his daughter, had made a lasting impression upon his mind.

"Welcome to Lichtenstein," said the old man, offering his hand, the grave features of his face giving place to a more kindly expression. "What are you standing gaping about there, you idle vagabonds?" he said to his servants, after the first salutation to his visitor; "do you suppose the gentleman is to lead his horse up into the room? Take him away to the stable, and bring his weapons into the saloon. I beg pardon, worthy sir, that these carles should have kept you so long waiting; but there is no beating sense into their thick heads. Will you follow me?"

He led on over the bridge, followed by Albert, whose heart beat in full expectation and longing desire to see and surprise his beloved. But recollecting the adventures of the preceding night, and the feeling which first prompted him to come to this spot, he blushed in shame for having suspected her fidelity. His eye sought all the windows in the hopes of seeing her; his ear was sharpened to catch if possible the sound of her voice: but in vain did his eye search the windows; in vain did his ear listen.

They had now reached the inner gate. It was strongly built, according to the ancient manner, with a portcullis, and openings above, to throw down boiling oil and water; and provided with all the other means of defence made use of in the olden times to repel a besieging enemy, should he have made himself master of the bridge. But it was not to the massive walls and fortifications alone which surrounded the castle that Lichtenstein was indebted for its security; nature claimed her share also in it. The rock itself formed a principal part of the habitation, having large roomy stables, and apartments which served as cellars, hewn out of it. A winding staircase led to the upper part of the castle, where military defences were likewise not less thought of than elsewhere. On the landing place, leading to the different rooms, and generally appropriated in similar habitations to the purposes of keeping the household utensils, were now to be seen match-guns, large chests containing shot, and divers other warlike weapons.1 The old knight's eye rested with a peculiar expression of pride upon this singular species of household furniture; and it is a fact that, in those days, the possessor of heavy artillery was accounted a man of opulence and wealth, for it was not every one who could afford to defend his castle with four or six such pieces as were possessed by the lord of the castle.

Another staircase led to the second story, upon which the knight of Lichtenstein showed his guest into a fine large saloon, lighted by several windows. He gave a sign to a servant who had followed them up, to withdraw.

FOOTNOTE TO CHAPTER XX.:

Footnote 1: There is a description, in an old chronicle, of Lichtenstein, as it existed at the end of the sixteenth century, about sixty years after 1519. It is stated therein, "In the upper story, there is a remarkable handsome room, surrounded on all sides by windows, from which may be seen the Asperg. The banished Duke Ulerich of Würtemberg, who often visited it, came every night to the castle, and saying, 'The man is here!' was immediately received." A gamekeeper's house is now built upon the ruins of the old castle, which still retains its name, and serves on Whitsunday as a place of rendezvous for the peasantry of the surrounding country, who assemble in their gayest dresses for dancing and carousal.

CHAPTER XXI

The noble spirit of the victim brave

Affects the knight, he feels that he must save;

The dews of friendship o'er his eyelids steal,

His heart no longer can resist th' appeal.

P. Conz.

When the two men were left alone in the saloon of Lichtenstein, the old knight gazed at Albert full in the face, with a scrutinizing eye, as if to satisfy himself of the honesty of his looks. The noble features of his visitor convinced him of the purity of his heart, and animated the old man's eye with a ray of joy. The air of melancholy which habitually sat on his brow had vanished, he became cheerful, he received Albert as a father would a son, who had returned from a long journey. A tear at length stole from his brilliant eye; but it was a tear of joy, for he pressed the astonished youth to his heart.

"It is not often that I am betrayed into this weakness," he said to Albert, "but in moments such as these nature gives way, because they happen seldom. Dare I indeed trust my old eyes? Do the contents of this letter deceive me? Is the seal really his? and can I believe it? but why do I doubt! has not nature stampt the impression of her noblest gifts upon your open forehead? Oh, yes, honesty is too visibly depicted on your countenance; you cannot deceive me; the cause of my unfortunate master has gained another friend!"

"If you allude to the cause of the banished Duke, you are not mistaken; it has found a warm partisan in me. Report has long since reached my ear of the knight of Lichtenstein being a faithful friend of his, and with this assurance I should perhaps have presented myself to you ere this, of my own accord, without the introduction of the unfortunate man in the cavern."

"Sit down beside me, my young friend," said the old man, who continued to regard Albert with a look of benevolence, "seat yourself, and listen to what I say: generally speaking, I am not an admirer of persons who change their minds. The experience of a long life has taught me to respect the opinion of others, and to assert that a man who entertains pure and honest views of a subject, is not therefore to be prejudged by another, who may think differently. But when a person changes his colours from real disinterested motives, as you appear to have done, Albert von Sturmfeder, and turns his back upon prosperity, for the noble purpose of allying himself to, and aiding the oppressed, in a just cause, then it is that his virtuous intentions justify his conduct, and carry along with them the stamp of a noble act."

Albert blushed for himself, when he heard old Lichtenstein praising his disinterested motives. Was it not for the sake of the beautiful daughter of the knight, that he had principally been induced to join his colours? and would he not sink in the esteem of this man, when, sooner or later, his real motive for embracing his party came to light? "You are too good," he answered; "the views of a man are often buried deeper than we at first sight think. But be assured, that though the step I have taken was dictated partly by a feeling which revolts at the idea of unjust oppression; I would not have you think too well of me, because it would give me very great pain, were you afterwards to be obliged to pronounce an unfavourable opinion upon my actions."

"I love you still more for your frankness," replied the lord of the castle, and squeezed the hand of his guest: "I can trust to my knowledge of physiognomy, and maintain, from what I see in yours, that, though other views may have influenced you, besides the feeling of justice, you never will be found wanting in honour. Whoever is led by evil intentions is a coward, and no coward would dare to run his head against Truchses, the Duke of Bavaria, and the whole Swabian League, and rise superior to the danger, as you have done."

"What do you know of me," said Albert, with joyful surprise; "have you ever heard of me before this moment?"

A servant, who opened the door at these words, interrupted the answer of the old man. He set a breakfast of game and a can full of wine before Albert, and prepared to wait on the guest; but a hint from his master made him withdraw. "Don't spare this morning's meal," said he to the young man; "the first glass, indeed, ought to be drank to the lady of the house, according to courteous habits; but mine has long departed this life, and my only daughter, Bertha, who acts in her place, is gone down to the village church, to hear the sermon and mass on this holiday. Well, you asked me if I have ever heard of you before? As you now belong to our party, I may venture to acquaint you with what I otherwise should have kept secret.

When you entered Ulm, I was also in the town, not only for the purpose of taking my daughter home, who was residing there, but principally to learn many things, which were important for the Duke to know. Gold opened all the doors," he added with a smile, "and unbolted those also of the grand council; by which means I became acquainted with everything the commanders of the League had determined upon. When war was declared, I was obliged to leave the place, but I left faithful men behind me in the town, who informed me of every circumstance, even the most secret."

"Was not the fifer of Hardt one of them," asked Albert, "whom I found with the exile?"

"Yes; the same who conducted you over the Alb." Albert started. "I had daily intelligence of the most secret affairs. Among other things, I learnt that they had determined to send a trusty spy into the neighbourhood of Tübingen, to gain intelligence and advertise the League of our movements. I heard you were selected for that service. I must tell you honestly, that, though you and your name were indifferent to me, for I did not know you personally, still I regretted that your young blood should be employed on that service, for, as sure as you live, the moment you had passed the Alb in the degrading character of a spy, so soon would you have been cut to pieces without grace or mercy. So much more surprising then was the information to me, when I learned further, that you had refused the service, and had spoken boldly before your employers. The fact also of your having renounced their party, and sworn to keep in a state of neutrality for fourteen days, was also made known to me. How much I rejoice then that you have become our friend also, I leave you to imagine!"

Nothing could have been more gratifying to Albert's feelings than the eulogium passed on his conduct by the knight of Lichtenstein. This moment removed all obstacles which had hitherto interrupted the tie between him and Bertha. The only wish of his heart, which he at times thought would never be realised, and had almost given up in despair, he now might hope would be accomplished, for he unknowingly had gained the good will of her father. "Yes, I renounced their service," he answered, "because their intentions outraged my feelings; I became your friend with heart and soul. When I was seated beside the exiled man in the cavern, and heard the disgraceful manner in which the lord of the land and the nobles were treated, I felt the force of his language strengthen my resolutions. In that moment all doubts and difficulties were removed from my mind, every thing was as clear as day, my only desire was, to draw my sword in this cause! And do you think we shall be called into action soon? How stand the Duke's affairs? You must not suppose I am come to you to set with my hands across."

"I can well imagine your anxiety to be in the field," said the old knight; "forty years ago I possessed the same ardour. You are aware, perhaps, in what state our affairs are at present; more upon the decline, I fear, than prosperous. The enemy is in possession of the whole tract of the low country as far up as Urach. Our fate depends upon one solitary circumstance,----if Tübingen holds out, victory is ours!"

"The honour of forty knights will, I think, answer for its safety," replied Albert, with animation; "the castle is strong, I have never seen a stronger; the garrison is sufficient for its defence, and forty men of noble blood will not surrender for a trifle. They cannot--they dare not. Have they not the children of the duke, and the treasures of his house, under their protection?--they *must* hold out."

"It were well if they were all like-minded with you," said the old man. "Tübingen holds a great stake in her hands. If the Duke can bring succour to its relief, he will then have a starting point, whence he will be able to reconquer his country. The place contains large supplies of munitions of war; and most of the nobility are assembled within its walls. So long as they remain faithful to his cause, so long will the feeling of Würtemberg be for the Duke, were he only to possess the spot upon which he stands; but I fear, I fear for the result."

"How? do you think it likely the knights will surrender? Impossible!"

"You have had but little experience in the ways of the world," replied the old man; "you are not aware of the many allurements and snares at work, which may make many a man waver in his allegiance. It is on this account, that the Duke, being doubtful of the fidelity of some of them in Tübingen, has sent Maxx Stumpf von Schweinsberg with a letter to the garrison written in strong terms, not only urging them to hold the castle to the last, but to afford him the means of entering therein himself, being ready to sacrifice his life in its defence, if God should so ordain it."

"Poor man," said Albert, moved by the consideration of the Duke's hard fate; "I cannot believe the nobility of the land will act in a manner unworthy of their rank. His presence among them will encourage their desponding hopes, sorties will be made, the besiegers will be beaten in spite of Bavaria and Fronsberg. We'll join them sword in hand, and drive these Leaguists out of the country."

"Maxx Stumpf is not yet returned," replied the knight of Lichtenstein, with a look of anxiety; "and the firing has ceased since yesterday. We hear every shot here on the Lichtenstein; but during the last twenty-four hours all is as quiet as the grave."

"Perhaps they have ceased firing on account of the holidays; you'll see that, to-morrow, or Easter Monday, they will re-commence with redoubled vigour, and make your rocks echo again."

"What is it you say?" replied the other, "on account of the holidays? To serve the Duke faithfully is a pious undertaking; and the saints in Heaven would perhaps rather hear the thunder of cannon in a just cause than that the knights should remain idle. Idleness is the parent of all vice! But, I trust, when Maxx arrives in the castle, he will rouse them out of their slumbers."

"Do you mean that the Duke had sent the knight of Schweinsberg to Tübingen, and that he intended to follow him, because the garrison has shewn symptoms of surrender? Has he not flown to Mömpelgard, as the people say? or is he still in the neighbourhood? Oh, that I could see him, and accompany him!"

A peculiar smile passed rapidly over the stern countenance of the old man. "You will sec him at the proper moment," he said; "he will be happy to see you also, for he loves you already. And, if fortune favours us, you shall also go with him to his castle, I give you my word. But for the present I must beg you will remain patiently alone for a short time; some business calls me, but it will be soon finished. I leave you in the company of some good old wine; make yourself at home in my house; were it not Good Friday, I would invite you to go out hunting." The old man pressed Albert's hand once more, and left the room; and soon after he saw him ride out of the castle towards the wood.

When the young man found himself alone, he commenced putting his dress in order, which in consequence of his recent adventures, required some attention. Whoever has been in the vicinity of the lady of his love, under Albert's circumstances, will not blame him for taking advantage of a piece of polished metal, which served as a looking-glass, hanging on the wall, to arrange his beard and hair. Having brushed his jacket, and removed all traces of having passed the night underground, he went into the large saloon, and sought among the many windows which surrounded it, the one which would give him the best view of the path leading up to the castle from the church of the village in the valley below, whither Bertha had gone to hear mass.

Cheering thoughts passed through his mind, in rapid succession, like bright vapours flying under the blue vault of heaven. He was now on the spot which had long been the object of his ardent desire to visit; he viewed the mountains and rocks which Bertha had often spoke about; he felt a charm in being in the same house which had been the dwelling of her childhood, and in which she had grown up to woman's estate.

Albert went into the small spot of ground within the walls of the castle, adorned with flowers, and which assumed the name of garden. Again his imagination wandered, in the pleasing supposition that it had been created by her orders; the flowers appeared to speak to him in her name--he was in the act of bending under a tree to pluck a violet, when he heard footsteps at the gate. He turned around to observe who it might be, it was indeed Bertha herself--she stood there wrapt in surprise and motionless, scarcely trusting her eyes. He flew to her, and pressed her to his heart; her astonishment at the unexpected apparition gave way to the conviction that it was really her lover, and not his spirit that embraced her. They had more to ask each other than they knew well how to answer in the first transport of joy, for they could with difficulty convince themselves that it was not a dream, thus to find themselves in each other's presence without fear or interruption. Having returned to the house, Bertha said,

"How much have I suffered on your account, dearest Albert; and with what a heavy heart did I leave Ulm! You had, indeed, sworn to quit the service of the League; but I had no hopes of seeing you so soon. And then, when Hans informed me, that, on your journey with him to Lichtenstein, you had been surprised by the enemy on the road, and dangerously wounded, my heart was almost broken, at the thought that I could not go to you and nurse you."

Stung with remorse for having given place to the jealousy which the story of the hostess of the Golden Stag at Pfullingen had created in his breast, he sunk in his own estimation before the tender love of Bertha. He sought to conceal his confusion, and related to her, amidst the interruption of her numerous questions, all that had happened to him since their separation; the cause which had favoured his quitting the service of the League with honour; the particulars of his perilous escape from the enemy's patrole; the kind care which the fifer's wife and daughter had taken of him, by which he was enabled to prosecute his journey to Lichtenstein.

Albert's conscience was too honest not to feel embarrassed at some of Bertha's scrutinising questions; and when she wished to have her curiosity satisfied upon the subject of his coming to Lichtenstein at so strange an hour of the night he scarcely knew what to answer. Her beautiful eye rested upon him with such an expression of inquisitive penetration, that, though he would gladly have escaped the reproach of harbouring a momentary idea of her want of fidelity, he would not for all the world tell her an untruth.

"I will own," he said, with a confused look, "that I was infatuated by the hostess at Pfullingen; she told me something about you, which I could not hear with indifference."

"The hostess? about me?" cried Bertha, smiling; "well, but what brought you, at that late hour of the night, to this place?"

"Never mind, dearest; we'll not think of it any more. I know I acted like a fool. The exiled knight has quite convinced me how wrong I was."

"No, no," she replied, earnestly, "I am not going to let you escape so cheap; what had that chatterbox to say about me? tell me immediately----"

"Well, then, I give you leave to laugh at me as much as you please: she told me you had another lover, who came to visit you every night, whilst your father slept."

Bertha blushed; indignation, and the inclination to smile at a ridiculous story, contended for the mastery on her expressive features. "Well, I hope," she replied, "you repelled the calumny with proper contempt, and left her house immediately. That was the reason, I suppose, of your arriving here so late, with the intention of passing the night under our roof."

"I honestly avow, I had no such thought. You know I was not quite convalescent, so excuse my weakness. I really did not believe her at first; but when she brought your nurse, old Rosel, to substantiate what she said, and who moreover lamented that I had been deceived, I----oh, do not turn away from me, Bertha; do not be angry! I threw myself on my horse, and rode direct to the castle, for the purpose of exchanging a word with him who dared to love you."

"And could you believe that?" she answered, with tears starting into her eyes: "I cannot think that Rosel said any thing of the kind, though she is fond of a gossip; I am not angry with the hostess, for she does not know better; but that you, you Albert, should give credit to so foul a falsehood, and think it necessary to convince yourself, that----" The tears of the faithful girl flowed in abundance; and the feeling of mortification choked her further utterance.

Her lover was overcome by the sense of his egregious folly; but he also felt the consolation, that though he was to be blamed his suspicions arose purely out of the intensity of his love. "Pardon me this once, dearest; let me assure you, that the jealousy which tormented me, unfounded as it was, would never have been inflamed into reality, did not my whole existence depend upon you."

"He who really loves can never harbour a spark of jealousy, founded upon such reports," said Bertha, in displeasure; "you hinted something of the same kind once before in Ulm, which you know hurt me very deeply. But if you had known me, and loved me with the same unalterable attachment that I love you, you never could have entertained such thoughts."

"No, truly, but you must not be unjust," he replied, and took her hand; "how can you reproach me with not returning your love with the same ardent sincerity? Was it impossible that one more worthy than Albert von Sturmfeder might appear, and supplant him in your heart by some infernal enchantment? Every thing is possible in this world."

"Possible!" interrupted Bertha; and a certain pride, which Albert had often remarked in the daughter of Lichtenstein, appeared now to animate her; "possible? if you ever could have entertained such an opinion of me,--I repeat it, Albert von Sturmfeder,--you have never loved me. A man must not allow himself to be blown about like a reed; he ought to stand firm to his opinion; and if he loves, he must have faith also."

"I have not merited such a reproach, from you at least," said the young man, starting up in great excitement; "I have been, indeed, as you say, a reed shaken about in the wind, and many a man will despise me----"

"That may be!" she whispered to herself, but not so lightly as to escape his ear, and cause his displeasure to blaze up into rage.

"Can you upbraid me thus," said he, "you, who are the sole cause of my vaccilating conduct? Did I not seek you among the friends of the League; and when I found you, was I not overjoyed? You entreated me to quit their colours,--I did so; and still more, I came over to your party, and, though it nearly cost me my life, I held firm to my determination. I visited your father, who received me as a son; and rejoiced that I had bound myself to the Duke's cause. But his daughter compares me to a reed moved by every blast of wind! but once more I will----for the last time, allow myself to be moved by you; I'll leave you, as you requite my love thus; in an hour hence, I wish you farewell." With these last words he girded on his sword; and, taking his cap, turned to depart.

"Albert," cried Bertha, with the sweetest accent, at the same time springing up and seizing his hand; her pride, her displeasure, every trace of ill-will vanished in a moment, and entreating love only beamed from her eyes, "for God's sake, Albert! I did not mean to speak so angrily; remain, I will forget every thing; I am ashamed of myself for having betrayed so unkind a spirit."

But the anger of the young man was not to be appeased in a moment. He turned away, lest her looks should master his resolution of leaving the castle. "No!" he cried, "you shall not turn the reed back again; but you may tell your father the cause which has driven his guest from his house." The windows trembled with the sound of his voice; he looked about him with wildness; he tore his hand away from Bertha's grasp; and, followed by her, he hastily opened the door to fly from her presence, when an apparition arrested his attention on the threshold which we shall describe in the next chapter.

CHAPTER XXII

Prince's favour, April's sky,

Woman's love, the rose's dye,

Cards, dice, and weathercocks are still

Chang'd about, believe't who will.

Old Proverb.

The apparition which so opportunely arrested the attention of Albert on opening the door, was no other than the old nurse, Rosel, hastily rising from a bent position she had taken up at the keyhole. She was one of those old servants, who, having been brought up in the family from her youth, was firmly rooted in it, and now formed one of its principal branches. Since the death of the Lady of Lichtenstein, Bertha's mother, she had shewn her attachment to the family in the assiduous care she had taken in bringing up her charge. Having passed through the different gradations, from nursery-maid to nurse, from nurse to housekeeper, she now occupied the more important post of governess and confidant to her foster-child. Greatly jealous of others, and ambitious to secure all authority in her own hands, she filled for many years the different important domestic situations of the castle, making herself universally necessary in all its concerns. Having gained an ascendancy over her master, who never found fault with her, at least before others, she gave out that she was essential in the management of the domestic affairs of the family, that without her superintendence, things could not go on right.

Of late, she had not lived on the best terms with her young mistress. In the days of her childhood and first youth, she had possessed her whole confidence. Even in Tübingen she was partly in the secret of Bertha's love; and old Rosel took such an interest in every thing that related to her child, as she always called her, as to speak in the first person plural, "*We* love Albert von Sturmfeder most tenderly,"--or "*Our* heart is ready to break in parting from him."

Two circumstances, however, tended to weaken this confidence. The young lady remarked, that her nurse was too fond of gossiping, that she had been even watching her movements, and had been twattling with others about her intimacy with Albert; she, therefore, grew more reserved towards the old woman, who very soon guessed the cause of it. But when the journey to Ulm was undertaken, and she had provided herself with a new woollen-stuff gown, and a superb brocade cap, upon the occasion, her disappointment knew no bounds upon being ordered to remain at Lichtenstein. This widened the breach between her and Bertha, for she attributed the cause of her not accompanying the family to her mistress.

Confidence between them was not restored after the knight of Lichtenstein returned with his daughter to the castle from Ulm. Old Rosel, who always preferred the society of her superiors to that of the domestics, endeavoured to obtain some information from Bertha about Albert, hoping thus to re-establish herself in her good graces; but Bertha, whose heart was then full of the late painful occurrences at the meeting with her lover, and still suspicious of the discretion of her nurse, would not satisfy her curiosity. When, therefore, the exile visited the castle at stated hours every night, and her young lady secretly prepared his meal, and, as her nurse thought, remained alone with him for a length of time, she gratified her pique towards her mistress by opening her heart to the hostess of the Golden Stag at Pfullingen upon the subject. No wonder, then, that Albert was led to believe every word he heard; because, having only known the nurse as the confidant of his love, he was not aware that the intimacy between her and Bertha had suffered interruption.

She had accompanied her mistress the morning of Albert's arrival, in her best Sunday's attire, to her pilgrimage to the church. Having confessed her sins, among which "curiosity" preponderated above the rest, and received absolution, she returned to Lichtenstein with a lighter heart and clearer conscience than she had when she left the castle, sighing under the weight of them. But the words of the father confessor had not probed so deep in her soul as to root out effectually her besetting sin, for when she got into her apartment and was occupied in putting by her rosary and Sunday dress, she heard her young lady and a man's deep voice in angry conversation together, and she even thought her mistress was crying.

"Can the nocturnal visitor have come up here in the day time, and taken advantage of the old man's absence?" she muttered to herself. A natural feeling of curiosity and sympathy drew her eye and ear involuntarily to the keyhole, when she overheard the dispute of which we have already been witnesses.

The young man opened the door so suddenly that she had no time to retreat, scarcely sufficient to recover her upright figure from her bending position. But she did not lose her presence of mind in this awkward predicament, for stopping Albert, and before either of them could speak, seizing his hands, poured upon him a torrent of words.

"Ay, upon my veracity! Could I ever have thought that my old eyes would have beheld Albert von Sturmfeder again! And I verily believe you have grown handsomer and taller than when I last saw you! Who could have thought it? Look, he stands like a stick at the door! Well, but who is it that dares speak thus to my dear young lady? It is not my master, nor any of his servants! Ay! what does one live to see? Young Albert, it is you who have been upbraiding my child!"

During this rapid flow of exclamations, Albert in vain sought to escape from the old woman, and though he determined, in the heat of the moment, to leave the castle, he felt it unseemly to let her suppose he had been quarrelling with Bertha. He shook off the grasp which the nurse had of him, and, in spite of her reproachful smile, took the hand of Bertha, at the same time pressing it to his heart. A glance from her eye calmed the tumult of his feelings. But a fresh conflict, a new embarrassment agitated him. His anger indeed subsided, he felt convinced that Bertha could not entertain that unkindness towards him which his heated imagination had conjured up--but how to reconcile it with his honour, to submit to the shame of being subdued by a squeeze of the hand, or a glance of the eye, before a witness, was a difficulty in which pride had its share. He blushed for his weakness, in standing self-convicted before the old woman; and we have often heard that the feeling of shame, and the embarrassment of getting out of a scrape, such as Albert's precipitation had drawn him into, without committing our honour, is apt often to convert a trifling quarrel into a lasting one, and dissolve ties founded on the basis of tender affection.

Old Rosel perceived with some degree of pleasure the anxiety and sorrow of her young lady, and would perhaps have gladly taken advantage of her distress, by way of punishing her for the withdrawal of her confidence, had not her natural kindness of heart resumed its sway over the malicious joy which she had given way too. She looked at the young man full in the face, and said, "You surely don't intend to leave us so soon, since it is but an hour ago that you arrived at Lichtenstein? Before you have had your mid-day meal, we will not allow you to depart, for that would be quite against the custom of the castle; and besides which, you have probably not yet seen my master?"

It was a great point gained for Bertha's cause to hear Albert speak again: "I have already spoken to him," he said; "as a proof of it, look at the two goblets we have emptied together."

"Well," continued the old woman, "but you would not leave his house without wishing him farewell?"

"No, I ought not certainly, as he desired me to wait for him in the castle," replied the young man.

"Aye, why would you go away in such a hurry, then?" she said, and forced him back into the room; "do you call that manners? My master would wonder, indeed, to think what kind of guest he had entertained. Whoever comes here by day," she added, with a searching look at Bertha, "whoever comes by broad daylight, possesses a clear conscience, and need not *slip away like a thief in the night.*"

Bertha blushed, and pressed the hand of her lover, who could not refrain from smiling, when he thought of the old woman's mistaken notion respecting the nocturnal visitor, and remarked the reproachful glance which she threw at her child.

"Yes, yes, as I said," she continued, "you have no occasion to steal away like a thief in the night. It had been better, perhaps, had you come sooner. The proverb says, 'judge for yourself, to doubt is dangerous, and he who seeks peace and quiet, let him remain with his cow!'--but I say nothing."

"Well, then," said Bertha, "you see he remains here; your proverbs are misplaced. You know, yourself, they do not always agree with the subject."

"Really? but they sometimes hit the right nail upon the head, however disagreeable it may be to the hearer. But repentance and good advice come too late after the evil has happened. I know well enough, that ingratitude is the wages of the world, and I can be silent! he who seeks peace and quiet, let him keep his eyes open, listen, and be silent."

"Come then, be silent," said Bertha, somewhat displeased; "at any rate it will be wise of you not to let my father remark that you know Albert von Sturmfeder; it were not unlikely he might suppose he is come to Lichtenstein for our sakes alone."

Good and ill humour strove for the mastery in old Rosel's breast. She was, on the one hand, flattered to be admitted again into her lady's confidence, by being requested to keep silence before her master, but, on the other, she still felt annoyed that her young mistress confided so little of her heart to her. She kept muttering a few indistinct words to herself, as she put the chairs in their places against the wall, and took the goblets off the table, wiping the marks which the wine had left on the slate slab with which the table was inlaid. Albert had retired to one of the windows, and though he did not feel quite reconciled to his love, yet he could not mistake a sign she gave him. He was particularly anxious her father should, as yet, know nothing of their mutual feeling, for he feared he might attribute to it the principal motive which had induced him to join Würtemburg's cause, and thereby lose the favourable opinion he had formed of him. Thinking it the wisest plan to pacify the old woman, he approached her, and tapping her gently on the shoulder, said, in a kind manner, "Miss Rosalie, you have a very pretty cap on, but the riband does not match it properly, it looks old and faded."

"Eh! what?" she answered in a pet, expecting to be addressed with more respect: "don't trouble yourself about my cap; every one has enough to do to sweep before his own door. Look first to yourself and your own affairs, and then find fault with me and mine. I am a poor woman, and can't dress like a countess. If all the world were alike, and all rich, and all sat at the same table together, who would you find to serve up the eatables and drinkables?"

"I did not mean to affront you," said Albert, and by way of soothing her, took a silver coin out of his purse, adding, "but Rosalie will do me a favour by changing her riband: and that my request may not sound unreasonable, she will not, I hope, refuse to accept a broad piece!"

Who has not seen the sun disperse the mists of a day of October? In like manner was old Rosel's ill-humour dispelled. The polite manner of the young knight, who had touched her weak point, by calling her Rosalie, her favourite name, instead of the familiar one of old Rosel, and presenting her with a dollar, having the bust of the Duke on one side, and the arms of Teck on the reverse, were charms too potent for her to withstand. "Ah, I see you are still the same good friendly gentleman," she said; whilst, stooping down, she glided the dollar into a large leather pocket which hung to her side, and carried the hem of Albert's cloak to her lips: "just so used you to do in Tübingen. When I stood at the fountain of St. George, or went from the hill down to the market place, I was sure to hear you call to me,--'Good morning, Rosalie; and how is your young lady?' And did you not often give me presents? why at least two thirds of the gown I wear comes from the bounty and kindness of your honour!"

"Never mind that now, good woman," said Albert, interrupting the old chatterbox; "But about your master,--you will not----"

"What do you mean?" she replied, half shutting her eyes: "I can pretend never to have seen you in my life. You may rest assured of that. That which does not burn I will not inflame!"

With these words she left the room and went down to the first floor, to attend to her affairs in the kitchen.

Grateful and full of joy, she took the dollar out of her leather pocket, and looked at it over and over again on both sides. She praised the liberality of the youth, and regretted that his love had been so ill requited, for that her young lady was unfaithful to him was a clear case in her eyes. She stood in the kitchen for some time wrapt in thought. She doubted within herself whether to let the thing take its course, or whether it would not be better to give a hint to the young knight, to apprise him of the nocturnal visitor. "But," she said, "in time of need comes help; perhaps he will see it himself, and does not want my advice. Besides, a meddler between two lovers is likely to burn his own fingers. It will be better to wait and look on, for heat in counsel and rashness in action engender nothing but harm. Who seeks peace and quiet, let him keep his eyes open, listen, and be silent!"

Such were the thoughts of the old philosopher in the kitchen. The lovers had in the mean time made up their differences. Albert was unable to withstand the entreaties of Bertha, and when she asked him, in the most tender tone, whether he was still angry with her, he could not bring his heart to say, yes. Peace was therefore re-established between them, and, which is seldom the case, in a shorter time than that which had been taken up in producing the dispute. She listened to the continuation of his adventures with great interest. It required, nevertheless, the conviction of his stedfast faith in her love, and in the word of the exiled man, to restrain his jealousy within due limits; for when he described his first encounter with his opponent, he observed a blush on her countenance, which raised a doubt in his mind whether it expressed joy for his escape from so formidable and experienced an adversary, or whether it was not occasioned by a lurking interest she took in the stranger. In relating further his visit to the exile in the dreary regions of his retreat, and all the circumstances connected with it, his admiration of the knight's noble mind, his greatness of soul amidst privations and miseries, tears started into her eyes, she looked up to Heaven as if in the act of imploring God's protection upon the unhappy man.

The conversation also which he had had with him, and particularly that part of it in which the exile addressed him as his friend, extolling his magnanimity for having pledged his faith to serve Würtemberg,--the cause of the oppressed and banished,--lighted up the glance of Bertha's eyes with unusual brilliancy. She gazed on her lover for some time in silent admiration. The sufferings she had endured since she last saw him were now effaced by the joy she felt in having him by her side as the staunch ally of her father. Albert was ashamed to feel his heart beat quicker at the interest Bertha appeared to take in everything relating to his new acquaintance. But he had command enough over himself to conceal his uneasiness from her, whilst his conscience upbraided him for harbouring the slightest suspicion of her fidelity.

"Albert," she said, "some time hence many a one will envy you this night's adventure. You may think yourself highly honoured, for it is not every one that Hans would venture to conduct to the exile."

"You know him, then?" replied the young man, eager to hear from her what he had failed to elicit from the fifer. "Oh, tell me who he is! I have seldom seen a man whose features, whose whole bearing, have acquired such an ascendancy over me? He told me he would at present be called by no other name than 'the man;' but his arm, whose strength I have felt, his penetrating look, convince me his name must be renowned in the world."

"He had a name, indeed, once," she answered, "which could vie with the most noble in the land. But if he did not tell it you himself, neither dare I pronounce it, because it would be against my word to do so. You must exercise your patience a little longer," she added, smiling, "difficult as it may be to restrain your curiosity."

"But why cannot you tell me," he interrupted her, "are not we one? Ought we to withhold anything from each other? Come, tell me, who is the man in the cavern?"

"Do not be angry. Look ye, if it were my secret only, you know I would not conceal it from you a moment, and you might with justice demand it of me; but, though I know it would be safe in your keeping, I dare not tell it,--I cannot break my word."

Though frankness beamed in her countenance, and not a spark of guile reigned in her heart, her refusal to satisfy Albert's wish irritated him, and he was on the point of taxing her with duplicity, when the door burst open, and an immense dog sprang into the room. Albert gave an involuntary start, having never seen so powerful a beast. The dog took up a position opposite to him, eyed him with a fierce look, and began to growl. His voice bore an ominous sound, whilst a row of white teeth, which he every now and then showed, might have startled the courage of the bravest man; one word from Bertha was sufficient to quiet and make it lay down at her feet. She stroked his beautiful head, from which his sharp eye first glanced inquisitively at her and then at the stranger. "It does everything but speak," she said, smiling; "it comes to warn me not to betray my friend."

"I have never seen so beautiful an animal! How proudly it carries his head, as if he belonged to an emperor or a king."

"It belongs to him, the banished," replied Bertha; "it came to stop my mouth."

"But why does not the knight keep him with him? Truly, such an arm as his, supported by a dog of this kind, might defy a host of enemies."

"It is a watchful beast," she answered, "and savage; if he kept it in the cavern, he would, indeed, be a certain protection. The cavern is so extensive that a man may remain concealed in its interior without fear of molestation. But if by chance any one entered it, a dog might easily betray him, for as soon as it heard a footstep no one could control it; he would begin to growl and bark, and attract the notice of his master's enemies; he therefore ordered it to remain here. The dog understands his duty, and I take care of him. It pines for his master, and you should see his joy when night comes; he knows then that his lord will soon visit the castle; and, when the drawbridge falls, and footsteps are heard in the court, it is impossible to hold him any longer, he would break a dozen chains to get to his side."

"A beautiful specimen of fidelity!" said her lover; "but exemplified by the man to whom this dog belongs in a still higher degree. Faithful to his lord, he prefers banishment and misery rather than betray his cause. It is a folly in me," Albert added; "I am aware that curiosity is not seemly in a man, but I long to know who he is."

"Have patience till the night," said the maiden; "when he comes I will ask him if I may tell you. I doubt not but that he will permit me."

"It is a long time to wait," said Albert; "and really I cannot drive his image out of my head. If you will not tell me, I'll ask the dog; perhaps he will be kinder than you."

"Well, try him," said Bertha, laughing; "if he can speak, I'll allow him to satisfy your curiosity."

"Hearken, you enormous beast," said Albert, turning to the dog, who looked at him attentively; "tell me, what is your master's name?"

The dog raised himself proudly up, opened his broad jaws, and roared out, in terrifying tones, "U--U--U!"

Bertha coloured: "Let's have no more of this nonsense," she said, and called the dog to her; "who would talk to a dog when in Christian society?"

Albert appeared not to heed her remark. "He said 'U,' good dog; I'll wager he has been trained to it! It is not the first time he has been asked what his master's name was?"

Scarcely had he pronounced the last words than the dog repeated his U--U--U! in a still harsher tone. Bertha coloured again, she made it come and lay down at her feet, scolding him in displeasure.

"Well, we have it now," said Albert, in triumph; "his master's name is U!" He recollected that the curious word on the ring which the exile had given him began with an U. It is extraordinary, thought he. "Is your master's name, perhaps, Uffenheim? or Uxhüll? or Ulm? or, by the bye,----"

"Nonsense! the dog has no other note than U. How can you plague yourself in trying to find out a meaning to it? But here comes my father. If you wish to conceal our love from him, do not commit yourself. I'll leave you now, as it would not be right to be found together."

Albert promised to be discreet, and once more embraced Bertha, an indulgence which was likely to be the last for some time, should the presence of her father render it impossible to see her again alone. The dog appeared to watch the movements of the loving couple with astonishment, as if he were really gifted with human sense. The first sound of the horse's feet on the drawbridge was the signal for separation, when Bertha left the room accompanied by the faithful animal.

CHAPTER XXIII

The Duke, so sad, can find no rest,

And dark reflections fill his breast;

"How far, alas! from me removed,

How much is sunk, the land I loved."

G. Schwab.

Good Friday and Easter Sunday passed away, and Albert von Sturmfeder still remained at Lichtenstein. The knight of the castle had invited him to continue his visit until the war should take some decided turn, which would afford him an opportunity to render the Duke important service. We may well suppose how willingly the young man accepted the invitation.

To be under the same roof with his beloved, always near her, occasionally to pass a few moments with her alone, and to be loved of her father, were privileges his fondest dreams had never anticipated. One circumstance only clouded these delights, and that was, a certain gloomy anxiety of expression which at times hung about the brow of Bertha's father. It appeared that he was not satisfied with the news which he received from the Duke and the theatre of war. Messengers came to the castle at different times of day, but they arrived and departed without the knight imparting to his guest the contents of their despatches. Sometimes Albert thought he even saw the fifer of Hardt in the dusk of the evening gliding across the bridge. Hoping to get some information from him, he once hurried down to meet him; but by the time he reached the bridge, no trace of him was to be found.

Feeling somewhat hurt by being left in total ignorance of the state of affairs, which he conceived he had a right to be informed of, after the decided part he had taken, he could not help saying to Bertha, "I have tendered my services unreservedly to the Duke's friends, in spite of their cause not being very prosperous. The man in the cavern and the knight of Lichtenstein have both shewn me much friendship and confidence, but only up to a certain point. Why should I not know what is going on at Tübingen? Why should I not be made acquainted with the Duke's operations? Am I only kept here as a forlorn hope? Why do they disdain my advice?"

Bertha endeavoured to console him, and succeeded at times by mild persuasion to drive such thoughts from his mind; but there were moments when they returned with double force, and particularly when he saw her father absorbed in the consideration of the state of affairs.

At length, on the evening of Easter day, he could contain himself no longer, and put a direct question to the old knight, asking him if their affairs were in danger, what was the state of the Duke's plans, and whether his services would not be called into action soon? But his patron, taking him kindly by the hand, answered, "I have long remarked, that your heart is ready to burst with impatience in consequence of your being denied a share in our labours and cares; but only have a little more patience; perhaps one day longer may decide many important subjects. What is the use of tormenting you with the uncertain intelligence which our messengers have lately brought? Your ardent young mind is not fitted to unmask intrigue, or to counteract artifice. When the crisis approaches upon which we can base our plans with safety, believe me you shall be a welcome member in council and action. All you need know at present is, that our circumstances are neither good nor bad, but that we shall soon be obliged to act with increased decision."

Albert gave the old man due credit for his reserve, but still he was anything but satisfied with his answer. He could not even learn the name of the exile, of whom Bertha had inquired the night preceding, when he came to the castle as usual, if he would allow her to make him known to their guest, but the only answer he gave was, "The proper moment is not yet arrived."

There was still another circumstance which offended Albert's *amour propre*. He had often made known to the knight of Lichtenstein the intense interest he took in the welfare of the exile, and what heartfelt pleasure it would give him to cultivate his further acquaintance; nevertheless, he had never once been invited to join the nocturnal visit of the mysterious guest. He was too proud to press the subject; he waited night after night in the expectation of being called in to speak to the man, but he waited in vain. He resolved therefore to see the stranger some night without an invitation, and for this purpose he sought a fitting opportunity. His room, which he was obliged to enter every night regularly at eight o'clock, overlooked the valley below, and was situated immediately opposite to the side on which the bridge was placed. It was therefore out of the question to see him coming from this position. The large room on the second floor, which was not far from his own, was locked every night, and consequently debarred him from satisfying his curiosity from thence. On the landing place, to which the doors of the different rooms led, there were indeed two windows looking towards the bridge, but as they were grated and stood high, the view from them was confined to the distant country, and there was no possibility of obtaining a sight of the desired spot. Nothing was left for him, therefore, than to conceal himself somewhere in order to gratify his curiosity. On the first floor the plan was impossible, because the many people living there would subject him to discovery. But when he examined the gateway and the stables, which were hewn out of the solid rock, he discovered a niche near the drawbridge, concealed behind the wings of the gate, which were only shut when an enemy was before the castle. This was the spot which appeared best suited to secure him from discovery, and which afforded room enough to enable him to observe what was going on. On the left of the niche the drawbridge joined on to the gate, the stairs which led up to the dwelling rooms were on the right, in front was the entrance passage, which every one must pass who came into the castle. Albert determined to slip into this position on the coming night.

At eight o'clock a page brought him his night lamp, and led him, as usual, to his apartment. The lord of the castle and his daughter kindly wished him good night. He entered his room, and dismissing his servant, who generally assisted him to undress, threw himself on his bed in his clothes. He listened attentively to each hour of the clock as it struck in the village, and whose sounds were wafted towards him by the night-breeze. He often closed his eyes, and at times fell into that state when it requires painful exertion to combat the power of sleep. His present object was sufficiently important to keep him on the alert, and prevent him losing the opportunity of satisfying his curiosity. Ten o'clock had long struck; all was as still as death in the castle. He jumped up, took off his heavy boots and spurs, threw his cloak over him, and cautiously opened the door of his room. He held his breath, fearing to make the least noise; the hinges of the door creaked--he stopped to listen whether any one had heard the treacherous sound. Every thing remained quiet; the moon threw a dim light on the landing place, and Albert thought himself fortunate she had not betrayed him a second time. He glided softly towards the winding stairs, and stopped again to listen if all was quiet; he heard nothing but the whistling of the wind, and the rustling of the oak trees on the further side of the bridge. He stepped carefully down the stairs. The least noise sounds louder in the depth and quiet of night than at other times; attention is awakened at the slightest movement, which would not be noticed in the day time. If his foot stepped upon a grain of sand, its grating sound went up the winding stairs, and startled him into the supposition that the whole house was on the alert. Having arrived at the first floor, he listened again, and heard nothing but the faint cracking of the dying embers on the hearth of the kitchen. At last he got to his destination, an expedition upon which he had expended a whole quarter of an hour's time, which otherwise was an affair but of a moment. He placed himself in the niche, and drew the wing of the gate closer to him, so that it fully covered his position. A fissure in the door was large enough to enable him to see distinctly every thing that passed. Nothing appeared to move in the castle, though he thought he heard light footsteps above him, which he supposed might be those of Bertha.

After waiting a tedious long quarter of an hour, the village clock struck eleven. This being the appointed time of the nocturnal visit, Albert directed all his attention to hear the stranger's approach. A few minutes after he heard the dog bark, when at the same time a deep voice from the other side of the ditch hailed, and said, "Lichtenstein!"

"Who comes there?" was answered from the castle.

"The man is there," replied the other voice, which sounded familiar to his ear as being the one he had heard in the cavern.

The watchman, an old man, came forth from a casemate hewn out of the rock, and opened the lock of the drawbridge with a large curiously wrought key. Whilst he was thus employed the dog came bounding down the stairs, whining and wagging his tail, and jumped upon the old man, as if to assist him in letting fall the bridge for his master to enter. Bertha shortly after descended with a lantern, and assisted him with her light, for it appeared he had some difficulty in opening the lock.

"Make haste, Balthaser," she whispered to the old watchman, "he has been waiting some time, it is cold outside, and the wind blows keen."

"I have now only to unfasten the chain, worthy lady," he answered; "you shall soon see how well my bridge falls. I have oiled the hinges, as you ordered me, so that they do not creak any more, and disturb Mrs. Rosel out of her slumbers."

The chains rattled in their ascent, the bridge sunk gradually into its place, and the banished man, enveloped in his coarse cloak, came across. Though his bearing was deeply engraven on Albert's mind, yet his strikingly bold features, his commanding eye, his open forehead, and the agile movements of his limbs, filled the young man anew with admiration.

The nocturnal guest assisted Balthaser, the doorkeeper, to draw up the bridge, with a power which appeared almost superhuman. When the old man had withdrawn to his sleeping place, Albert overheard the following conversation between the visitor and Bertha.

"Is there any news from Tübingen? Has Maxx Stumpf returned? I read bad news in your countenance."

"No, sir, he has not yet returned," she replied; "my father expected him this very night."

"Oh, that the devil would give him heels! I must remain here till he comes, if it be for a whole day. Ha! a cold night, lady," said the exile; "the screech owls will be frozen in the cavern, for I left them crying in most pitiable tones."

"Yes, it is indeed cold," she answered; "I would not go down there, upon any account; and how dreadful must it be to hear those cries; I shudder to think of it."

"If young Albert accompanied you, you would have no objections to go," answered the other smiling, and chucking the blushing girl under the chin; "is it not so? You would not hesitate to follow him there, much as you appear to dread it now."

"Ah! sir," she replied, "how can you talk in that way? Do you know, I'll not come down again to let you in if you take such liberties."

"Well, but I merely spoke in jest," said the knight, and gently pinched her glowing cheek; "you know how little opportunity I have in my dwelling to enjoy a joke. What will you give me to say a good word to your father, to induce him to make the youth your husband? You are aware the old gentleman does every thing I ask him; and if I recommend a son-in-law to him, he would accept him at all hazards."

Bertha opened wide her beautiful eyes, and cast a grateful look at him. "Dear sir," she answered, "I will not forbid your saying a kind word for Albert, particularly as my father is well inclined towards him."

"But I shall expect some reward for my trouble. Everything has its price; so what will you give?"

Bertha cast her eyes to the ground. "A heartfelt thank-ye," she replied; "but come, sir, my father has been waiting for us a long time."

She was in the act of leading on, when the knight, taking her by the hand, detained her. Albert's heart beat so hard as almost to be heard; he broke out into a violent heat, and then became ice-cold; he laid hold of the handle of the door, and was on the point of sallying forth to forbid the promise of a fixed price being given upon any pretext.

"Why are you in such haste?" he heard the man of the cavern say. "Well, for one kiss only, and I will persuade your father to send for the priest on the spot, to perform the holy ceremony." He bent his head towards the offended, blushing girl. Albert saw every thing swimming before his eyes, and was again on the point of bursting from his place of concealment, but the determined reply of his lady love checked him from taking the rash step. She beheld the man with a forbidding look. "It is impossible your Grace can be in earnest," she said; "otherwise you now see me for the last time."

"If you knew how much this scornful air becomes you," he answered, with unaltered kindness, "you would never cease to be in anger. At any rate I admire your fidelity; for when the heart is deeply engaged with one object, none other need hope for such a favour. But on your marriage day I will demand the favour, with the permission of your bridegroom, and then we'll see who is right."

"That you may do," said Bertha, smiling, whilst she withdrew her hand from his, and led the way with the light in her hand; "but you had better prepare yourself for a refusal, for he is not fond of trifling on this point."

"He is uncommonly jealous," replied the knight, as they proceeded up stairs. "I could tell you something upon that subject, which took place between him and me; but I promised silence----"

The sound of their voices died away gradually, and at last became indistinct to Albert's ear. He breathed freely again. He listened and remained in his position until he satisfied himself thoroughly that no one was on the stairs or in the passages, and, taking advantage of the opportunity, slipped up into his own room much quicker than he had descended from it. The last words of Bertha and the exile still resounded in his ears. He blushed to think of his unfounded jealousy, which had again tormented him this night. Bertha had, unknown to herself, given him evident proofs of the purity of her heart and faithful attachment to him; and it was only when he laid his head on his pillow and fell to sleep, that his mind was eased of the pain of having unjustly suspected her.

When he left his room the next morning at seven o'clock, the hour which the family generally assembled at breakfast, Bertha met him on the landing place with the appearance of having been weeping. She took him on one side, and whispered, "Tread softly, Albert; the knight of the cavern is still with us; he has been asleep about an hour; we must not disturb him."

"The exile!" asked Albert in astonishment, "does he dare remain here during the day? what has happened? is he unwell?"

"No!" answered Bertha, whilst a fresh tear hung on her eyelid, "no! he expects a messenger from Tübingen about this time, and is determined to await him. We begged and prayed him to depart before daybreak, but he would not listen to our warning, so firm is his resolution to remain at all hazards."

"But could not the messenger have gone to him in the cavern?" said Albert; "he runs too great a risk unnecessarily."

"Ah! you don't know him; it is his bane when he once gets a thing into his head to be obstinately immoveable; and then he is so distrustful of others, even of his best friends. It was quite impossible for us to persuade him to leave the castle this morning, because he might have thought, perhaps, we wished to get rid of him for our own safety. His principal reason for remaining is, I believe, to consult with my father, when the messenger arrives."

During this conversation they remained stationary on the landing place, but Bertha now opened the door of her father's apartment as gently as possible, and they entered together.

This room, or what would be called in a modern establishment the gentlemen's room, was distinguished from the saloon on the second floor from being somewhat smaller. It had a view of the surrounding country on three sides, through small round windows, now pierced by the sun's morning rays. The ceiling and walls were wainscoted with dark brown wood, fancifully inlaid with other coloured woods. A few portraits of the ancestors of Lichtenstein graced the side of the wall opposite to the windows, and the tables and furniture shewed that the present occupier of the castle was a friend of old customs and times, and that his property would descend to his daughter in the same unaltered state it had been left by his great-grandfather.

The old knight was seated at a large table in the middle of the room when they entered. Supporting his long-bearded chin in his hand, he sat gloomy and motionless, with his eyes fixed on a large goblet which stood before him. It was not quite evident to Albert whether he had been sitting up all night over his glass, or whether he was taking a draught at this early hour of the morning to recruit his strength and spirits.

He saluted the young man as he approached the table by a slight inclination of the head, whilst a scarcely visible smile played about his mouth. He pointed to a goblet on the table and a stool by his side. Bertha understanding the hint, filled it with wine, and presented it to her lover, with that grace which marked every thing she did. Albert seated himself beside the old man, and drank.

The latter drew his chair near to him, and said in a low tone of voice, "I fear our affairs are in a bad way!"

"Have you had any intelligence?" asked Albert, in the same low tone.

"A peasant told me this morning, that Tübingen had treated with the League last evening."

"Good heavens!" said Albert, involuntarily.

"Keep quiet, and do not wake him! he will learn it soon enough," replied the old man, pointing to the other side of the room.

The young man looked that way. At one of the side windows, looking towards the deep ravine, sat the exile asleep; his arm, resting on the ledge of the window, supported his careworn brow. His grey cloak had partly fallen off his shoulder, and discovered a worn-out leather jerkin, in which his powerful frame was encased. His curly hair hung down over his temples in disorder, and a few tufts of his smooth beard were visible from under his hand. The large dog lay at his feet, his head resting on his master's foot, looking up at him with faithful eyes and watching every motion of his features.

"He sleeps," said the old man, and repressed a starting tear. "He breathes light; oh! that his dreams may be comforting. The reality of life to him is melancholy indeed! Who can help wishing he may remain unconscious of it awhile?"

"His is a hard fate!" replied Albert, casting his eye at the sleeping man. "Driven from house and home--an outcast--a price offered to any villain who chooses to level his gun at him--under the earth by day, and by night wandering about like a thief! Truly, it is hard; and all this because he is faithful to his lord!"

"That man has suffered much in his lifetime," said Lichtenstein, with a serious look. "I have known him from the days of his childhood, and I can vouch for his having always wished to do what is right and just. The means indeed he applied to attain his object were at times not fitted to further his purpose; on other occasions his intentions were misunderstood, and he too often allowed himself to be carried away by the violence of passion--but where lives the man of which this might not be said? Truly, he has wofully repented himself." He stopt short, fearing he had said more than he ought before Albert, who asked in vain to hear something further of his character. The old man sank into silence and deep thought.

The sun having risen over the mountains and dispersed the mist which hung about the vallies, invited Albert to the window to enjoy the splendid view. A lovely valley, surrounded by wooded heights, with three smiling villages scattered over its surface, and a rapid stream running through it, lay at the foot of the rock of Lichtenstein. It was like beholding the earth from a point in the heavens. Leaving the valley and looking to the wooded heights, his eye rested with delight upon picturesque groups of rocks and the mountain of the Alb, behind which rises the castle of Achalm, and forms the boundary of the immediate surrounding country. Beyond the walls of Achalm, the distant hills were visible to the right and left. The rock of Lichtenstein, reaching, as it were, into the clouds, commands an extensive view of Würtemberg, free and unbroken, into the far lowland. The morning sun throwing its oblique rays across the landscape, Albert was transported with the beauty of its scenery.

The fertile fields spread before him, surrounded by the wooded hills, he compared to variegated carpets, edged, as it were, with borders of dark green and brown, deriving their different shades and colours from the tints thrown over them by the dawning day. And then turning to the country between Lichtenstein and the distant Asperg, he exclaimed, "What charms for the lover of the picturesque! No continuous uninterrupted plain to weary the beholder, the eye ranges from hill to mountain in pleasing variety, and rests on the luxuriant valley, with its meandering stream gently rippling along in its course."

Albert stood wrapt in delight. He strained his eyes more and more to see and distinguish each castle and village in the far distance. Bertha stood beside him, and though she had enjoyed the same view from her childhood, she now shared his pleasure; she pointed out every place, and named all the different towers to him. "Where is there another spot in all Germany which can be compared to this!" said Albert; "I have seen vast plains, and mounted heights which command perhaps a more extended view, but such a rich combination of the picturesque and the sublime it would be difficult to find elsewhere. Look at the rich corn fields, the woods of fruit trees, and a little lower down there, where the hill assumes a blueish tinge, that garden of vines! I have never yet envied a prince; but to stand here, and look over those hills, and say this is mine, would be the height of my ambition!"

A deep sigh close to them, started the young couple from their observations. They turned round, and perceived the exile standing at the window a few paces from them. He appeared to view the country with a wild look, which made Albert uncertain whether the conversation he had just had with Bertha, or the thought of his own forlorn state, had troubled his mind.

He saluted the young man, and offered him his hand, and turning to the lord of the castle, asked him, "If a messenger had arrived?" "Schweinsberg is not yet returned," he answered.

The exile retired again to the window in silence. Bertha filled him a goblet of wine. "Be of good courage," she said, "and don't look in so disconsolate a manner over the country. Drink this wine, it is good old Würtemberger, and grows under that blue mountain."

"We cannot remain long melancholy," he answered, and turned to Albert with a forced smile, "when the sun shines so cheerfully over Würtemberg, and Heaven's mildness beams in the eye of one of her fairest maidens? Is it not so, young man? what is the sight of these hills and vallies, compared to the gleam of such eyes and the fidelity of true hearts? take your glass, and let us drink to them! Nothing is irrevocably lost so long as we possess such treasures: here's to 'Good Würtemberg for ever!'"

"Good Würtemberg for ever," replied Albert, and touched glasses. The exile was going to say something more, when the old watchman entered with a face full of importance. "There are two pedlars before the castle, and demand admittance," he announced.

"It's them! it's them!" cried the exile and old Lichtenstein in the same breath, and added, "shew them up."

The servant withdrew. An anxious moment followed the announcement. No one said a word. The knight of Lichtenstein looked as if he could pierce the door with the eye of impatience. The exile endeavoured to conceal his anxiety, but the rapid changes on his expressive features indicated clearly that his whole being was in a state of excitement. At length footsteps were heard on the stairs approaching the apartment. The exile, strong as he was, trembled so much that he was obliged to hold by the table, his body was bent forward, his eye was fixed on the door, as if he would read his fate on the countenance of the messengers--the door opened and they entered.

CHAPTER XXIV

Deserted as thou art, by all forsaken,

Thy fortunes ruin'd and thy power gone,

Thou still shalt find fidelity unshaken,

Although you find it in myself alone.

Thy humble vassal, 'till the hour of death,

I'll hail my sovereign with my latest breath.

L. Uhland.

Albert's expectation was also raised to the highest pitch. His eye examined the two men as they entered, and he at once recognised the fifer of Hardt as one, and the pedlar he had met at the Golden Stag of Pfullingen as the other. The latter disburthened himself of a pack which he carried on his back, tore a plaister from his eye, erected himself from a bent position, which he had assumed for the purpose of disguise, and stood before the assembled group, the short-set, strong-built man, with open bold features, which the exile had already described in the cavern.

"Maxx Stumpf!" cried the exile in a trembling tone of voice, "what means that gloomy countenance? You bring us good news, don't you? they will open the gates to us, and with us hold out to the last man?"

Maxx Stumpf von Schweinsberg looked about him in confusion. "Prepare for the worst, sir!" he said, "the intelligence I bring you is not good."

"How?" answered the other, whilst the blush of rage flew into his cheeks, and the veins of his forehead began to swell, "how, do you mean they hesitate, they waver? It is impossible! be not precipitate in what you say, recollect it is of the nobles of the land of whom you speak."

"And still I will say it," Schweinsberg answered, making a step forward. "In the face of the Emperor and the Empire, I will say they are traitors."

"Thou liest!" cried the exile with a terrible voice. "Traitors, did you say? Thou liest! Dost thou dare to rob forty knights of their honour? Ha! own it, that you lie."

"Would to God I were a knight without honour--a dog that betrays his master! But the whole forty have broken their oaths--you have lost your country. My Lord Duke, Tübingen is gone!"

The man, whom these words more immediately concerned, sank in a chair at the window: he covered his face with his hands, his agitated breast appeared to seek in vain for breath, his whole frame trembled.

The eyes of all were directed to him, expressive of commiseration and pain, particularly Albert's, who now for the first time learnt the name of "the man"--it was him, Duke Ulerich of Würtemberg! Recollections of the first moment he had met him, of his first visit to the cavern, of the conversation they had had, and the way which his whole bearing had surprised him and bound him to his cause, crossed his mind in *one* rapid flight. It was quite incomprehensible to him, that he had not long ago made the discovery.

No one dared to break the silence for some time. The heavy breathing of the Duke only was heard, and his faithful dog, who appeared to partake of his master's misery, added his pitiable whining to the distressing scene. Old Lichtenstein at length giving a sign to the knight of Schweinsberg, they both approached the Duke, and touched his cloak, in order to rouse him, but he remained immoveable and silent. Bertha had stood aloof, with tears in her eyes. She now drew near with hesitating step, put her hand on his shoulder, and, beholding him with a look of tender compassion, at last took courage to say, "My Lord Duke! it is still good Würtemberg for ever!"

A deep sigh escaping from his breast, was the only notice he took of the kind girl's solicitude. Albert then approached him. The expression which the exile had made use of, when they first met, flashed across his mind, and he ventured to address the same words now to his afflicted friend. "Man without a name," said he, "why so downhearted? Si fractus illabatur orbis, impavidum ferient ruinæ!"1

These words acted like a charm upon Ulerich. Whether he had adopted them as his motto, or whether it was that combination of greatness of soul, and obstinate contempt of misfortune, which formed his character, and acquired for him the name of the "Undaunted," he was reanimated, as if by an electric spark, when he heard them repeated, and from that moment rose worthy of his name.

"Those are the true words, my young friend," he said at length with a firm voice, proudly raising his head, his eyes sparkling with their usual animation, "those are the words. I thank you for bringing them to my mind. Stand forward, Maxx Stumpf, knight of Schweinsberg, relate the result of your mission. But first of all, give me another glass, Bertha!"

"It was last Thursday, when I left you," began the knight: "Hans disguised me in this garb, and instructed me how to comport myself. I went to the Golden Stag at Pfullingen, just to try if any one would recognise me in it, but the hostess brought me a can of wine with all the indifference she would have done to a perfect stranger she had never seen before. And a city counsellor, with whom I had exchanged angry words not a week before in the same room, drank with me, supposing I had followed the vocation of pedlar from my childhood. That young man," pointing to Albert, "was also in the room."

The Duke appeared to recover his spirits, and was more cheerful. He asked Albert whether he had noticed the knight in his garb of pedlar, and whether he looked the character?

He replied, smiling, "I think he played his part to perfection."

"From Pfullingen I went the same evening to Reutlingen. I entered the public room of an inn, where I met a tribe of Leaguists, consisting of citizens, from all parts, who were exulting with the Reutlingeners, for having torn down the stag horns, the emblems of your house, from their city gates. Though they abused you and sang burlesque songs at your expense, still they appeared to fear your name. On Good Friday I proceeded towards Tübingen. My heart beat high when I descended through the wood near the castle, and saw the beautiful valley of the Neckar before me, with the fortified towers and steeples of that place peering above the hill."

The Duke compressed his lips, turned away, and looked at the distant country. Schweinsberg paused, sympathising in his master's pain, who beckoned to him, however, to proceed.

"Descending into the plain, I wandered onward towards Tübingen. The town had been already occupied by the League some days, the castle still held out, and only a few troops remained in the camp, which was pitched on the hill overlooking the valley of Ammer. I determined to slip into the town, for the purpose of finding out how affairs stood in the castle. You know the little inn in the upper town, not far from the church of St. George? I went there, and called for wine. On my way I learned that the knights of the League often assembled in the same house, and therefore I considered it the best place to attain my object."

"You risked a good deal," interrupted the knight of Lichtenstein: "it was very possible some one might have wished to buy some of your wares, and then the pedlar in disguise would have been discovered."

"You forget it was a holiday," replied the other, "so that I had a good excuse not to open my pack, and recommend my goods for sale, according to the custom of pedlars. But I had sufficient proof of the security of my disguise, for I sold a box of healing plaster to George von Fronsberg, God knows, I would gladly have come to blows with him, and given him an opportunity on the spot to make use of it. They were still at high mass in the church, and no one in the inn; but I learned from the master of the house, that the knights in the castle had agreed to a truce till Easter Monday. When church service was over, many knights and other men came, as I expected, into the room where I was, for their morning's potation. I seated myself in a corner on the bench near the stove, the proper place for people of my condition in the presence of their superiors."

"Who did you see there?" inquired the Duke.

"I knew some of them by sight, and guessed who others were from their conversation. There was Fronsberg, Alban von Closen, the Huttens, Sickingen, and many others. Truchses von Waldburg came in shortly after. When I saw him enter, I drew my cap deep over my face, for he cannot have forgotten the whirl I gave him from his horse some fifteen years ago by a thrust of my lance."

"Did you see Hans von Breitenstein among the rest?" asked Albert.

"Breitenstein?--not that I know; ah! yes, that's his name who will eat a leg of mutton at a sitting. Well, they began to talk of the siege and the truce, and some of them whispered to each other, but as I have very good ears, I heard just what of all things was most essential to know. Truchses related that he shot an arrow into the castle, with a note attached to it, addressed to Ludwig von Stadion. It appears that he must often have practised the same device, for the knights were not astonished, when he added, that he had received an answer the same day by similar means."

The Duke's countenance became clouded. "Ludwig von Stadion!" he cried in agony; "I would have staked castles upon his fidelity! I loved him so, that I satisfied all his desires, and he is the first to betray me!"

"The answer said, that he, Stadion, with many others, being tired of the contest, were more than half inclined to surrender; George von Hewen, however, threatened to denounce them as traitors."

"I have not merited such friendship from Hewen," said Ulerich. "I was once offended with him, for having complained that I had not acted according to his wishes. But how easily are we deceived in the characters of men! Had any one asked me which of these two I had most faith in, I would have named Stadion as my trusty friend, and George von Hewen the doubtful one."

Schweinsberg continued. "The answer also said, that your Grace would probably attempt to relieve the castle; but if that were impossible, you would repair to it in person by some secret way. The Leaguists spoke much upon that subject. They all, however, agreed that it was essential to bring the garrison to terms without delay, before you brought relief, or got into the castle; for if you succeeded in the latter case, they feared the siege might last much longer. After hearing all this, I did not think it advisable to proceed immediately to the castle by the secret path, known only to a few, and shew myself to the garrison, because if Stadion had already gained the upper hand, I should have been lost. I resolved, therefore, to remain the day in the town; and if before Saturday morning I heard nothing to alarm me respecting the spirit of the garrison, then to proceed to my destination, and send your Grace immediate intelligence. I wandered about the town and the camp unmolested until noon, seeking as much as possible always to be near some of the superior officers to assure myself of my disguise."

"That was on the Friday, the holiday?" Lichtenstein asked.

"Yes; on holy Friday. At three o'clock in the afternoon, George von Fronsberg, with many other of the principal officers, rode to the city gate of the castle; and hailed the besieged, inquiring whether they were building a fortification. I was standing among them; and saw Stadion come on the wall, and answer, 'No, that were against the terms of the truce; but I see,' he added, 'you are erecting a fort in the field.' George von Fronsberg cried, 'If it is so, it is without my orders. Who are you?' He in the castle answered, 'I am Ludwig von Stadion;' upon which the Leaguists smiled, and stroked their beards. Having satisfied the besieged, by overturning a few baskets filled with earth, which had been placed in the entrenchments to screen their works, that he had no knowledge of its having been done, Fronsberg then called to Stadion, and invited him, with other of his party, to come down and drink together."

"Did they go?" cried the Duke, impatiently, "and forget their honour?"

"There is an open space on the castle hill beyond the ditch, whence the spectator, having a distant view of the country, can survey the valley of the Neckar, the Steinlach on the height above, the Alb in the distance, with many castles and villages, which complete the scenery. On this spot they placed a table and benches; and the commanders of the League sat down to drink. The gate of Upper Tübingen was then opened, the bridge fell over the ditch; when Ludwig von Stadion, with six others, came forth, bringing with them your Grace's silver covered jugs, golden goblets, and best wine; and having saluted your enemies with a shake of the hand, seated themselves to talk over the state of affairs over a cool tankard."

"May the devil bless them all!" interrupted the old knight of Lichtenstein, and threw his wine away; but the Duke smiled, and nodded to Maxx Stumpf to proceed.

"They caroused together till after dusk; and staggered about with heated heads. I kept near them, so that not one of their traitorous words escaped my ears. When they broke up, Trachses took Stadion by the band, 'Brother,' said he, 'you have good wine in your cellar; let us in soon, that we may help you to drink it out.' The other laughed, shook him by the hand, and said, 'Time will teach us what to do.' When I saw how affairs stood, I determined, with God's help, at the risk of my life, to get into the castle: I therefore left them, and went to the spot where the secret subterranean way commences. Having succeeded in entering it unnoticed, and reached the middle, I found the portcullis down, with a sentry placed there. He levelled his gun at me, when he heard me coming in the dark, and demanded the parole. I gave, as you desired me, 'Atempto,' the watch-word of your brave ancestor, Eberhard with the beard. The fellow opened his eyes wide, drew up the portcullis, and let me pass. With rapid steps I reached a vault, where I was obliged to remain a few moments to take a breath of fresh air, for the narrow passage is close and damp."

"Faithful Maxx! clear your throat with a draught of wine," said Ulerich; the knight followed his advice, and continued his story with renewed vigour.

"I heard the sound of many voices in the vault, apparently in contention, and following its direction, I saw a number of the garrison sitting round a large cask drinking. There were some of Stadion's party, with Hewen, and many of his friends. The light of a lamp illumined their position, and the large goblets which were placed before them. It was an imposing scene, and put me in mind of a sitting of the secret tribunal. Having concealed myself behind a cask, I listened to their conversation. George von Hewen spoke stirring words, and represented to them the crime of their infidelity; he said there was no reason why they should surrender; that they were well provided with provisions for a long siege; that your Grace was assembling an army for their relief; and that the besiegers were worse off than themselves."

"Ha! brave Hewen! and what gave they for answer?" said the Duke.

"They only laughed and drank. 'It will be long before he can get an army together. Where will he find money, unless he plunders?' said one of the party. Hewen continued: 'But if the Duke cannot succeed so soon as he expected, we are nevertheless bound by our oath to hold to the last, or else be held as traitors to our lord and master.' They laughed and drank again, saying, 'Who dares come forward and call us traitors?' I then called out from behind my cask, 'I will! You are traitors--false to your oaths, to the Duke, and your country!' They were terrified and thunder-struck; Stadion let fall his goblet; when, stepping forward, having first taken off my disguise, I stood before them, and drew your letter from under my jerkin: here is a writing from your Duke, said I; he commands you at your peril to surrender; he is coming himself to conquer or die under the walls."

"Oh, Tübingen!" said the Duke, with a sigh, "fool that I was to leave you in such hands. I would give two of my left fingers for your sake! what did I say, two fingers? I would willingly lose my right hand could I purchase you with the sacrifice, and with my left lead the way to the heart of my enemies. And what was the answer to my words--did they not give any?"

"The false ones eyed me with sullen looks, and appeared not to know what to do. Hewen, however, repeated his warning to them. Stadion at last said, You come too late. Twenty-eight knights have determined to withdraw from the contest, and leave the Duke to settle his affairs alone with the League. If he returns to the country with an army they will faithfully stand by him, but they cannot continue to carry on the war any longer in a state of uncertainty as to the result, seeing that their opposition to the League has only subjected their houses and estates to damage and heavy contributions. I then requested to be led to the hall of the knights, where I would try to discover whether there were not still left honourable men sufficient to defend the castle. I reckoned upon the fidelity of the two Berlichingens, and many others, whose names are familiar to your Grace, as having sworn allegiance to your colours. But Hewen shook his head, and said I was mistaken in most of them."

"But Stammheim, Thierberg, Westerstetten, in whose faith I would have staked my existence--did you see them?" asked the Duke.

"Oh, yes! they were in the cellar with Stadion, and assisted to drink your wine. They would not allow me to go up into the castle. Even Hewen, with Freiberg and Heideck, who were with him, dissuaded me from it, because, they said, the two parties were already much inflamed against each other, Stadion having the majority of knights, and of the soldiers also, on his side. 'If I went up,' they added, 'and it should come to blows in the court of the castle, and in the hall of the knights, there would be nothing left for them, as the weakest party, than to fight for life and death. Willingly as they would shed their last drop of blood for you, they would rather fall before the enemy in the field of battle than be cut to pieces by their own countrymen and brothers in arms. Being foiled in every thing, I asked them, as a last petition, to protect your son, the young Prince Christoph, and your darling daughter, and preserve the castle to them, when they surrendered. Some of them consented, others remained silent, and shrugged up their shoulders. Exasperated, I denounced them as traitors, and giving them my curses as a Christian knight, challenged any five of them to fight with me for life and death when the war should be ended. Upon which I left them, and returned the same way out of the castle that I entered it."

"Würtemberg's honour is gone! could I have thought it possible!" cried Lichtenstein. "Forty-two knights, two hundred soldiers, thus to betray a fortified castle! Our good name is defamed,--futurity will brand with scorn our nobility, who deserted their Duke's banners. The saying 'faithful and honourable as a Würtemberger' is become a term of reproach."

"We could, indeed, once boast of the truth of the saying, 'faithful as a Würtemberger,'" said Duke Ulerich, whilst a tear fell on his beard. "When my ancestor Eberhard once upon a time rode towards Worms, and sat at table with the electors, counts and lords, each prided himself upon the pre-eminence of his own country. One boasted of his wine,--another spoke of his fruits,--a third of his game,--whilst a fourth talked of the metals which his mountains produced,--but, when it came to Eberhard with the Beard to speak, he said, 'I know nothing of your treasures, but this I know, that if I seek shelter in a humble peasant's cot, in the most secluded spot, tired and oppressed with fatigue, I am sure to find a faithful Würtemberger at hand, upon whose lap I can lay my head in safety and sleep in peace.' They all wondered in astonishment, and said, 'Count Eberhard is right, and long live the faithful Würtemberger!' But in these times behold, when the Duke traverses a wood, they lie in wait to kill him; and, if he places his faith in his nobles for the defence of his castles, scarcely does he turn his back but they treat with the enemy. May the cuckoo take such faith! But go on, Maxx, I am the man to drink the dregs of the cup without the fear of seeing the bottom of it."

"Well, it's soon said. I remained in Tübingen until I had convinced myself of its surrender. Yesterday, being Easter Monday, they came to terms; they drew up the articles in writing, and proclaimed throughout the streets by a herald, that, at five o'clock in the evening, the garrison would march out. Prince Christoph, your young son, retains the castle and administration of Tübingen, but in the service and under the guardianship of the League; and as for the rest of the country, it is said, that it will be divided among the knights. I have experienced many misfortunes in life,--I killed a friend at a tilting bout,--I have lost a dear child, and had my house burnt,--but, as true as God and his saints are gracious to me, I never felt so much pain as at that moment when I saw the banner of the League hoisted in lieu of your Grace's, and their red cross cover Würtemberg's stag horns, and bugle."

So spake Maxx Stumpf von Schweinsberg. The sun had risen, during his narration, high above the mountains, having dispelled the mists, leaving only a slight vapour on the heights of the Asperg. It hung upon the horizon like a thin veil, and heightened the beauty of the scenery in its immediate neighbourhood. Drest in the soft verdure of spring, combined with the darker foliage of the woods, ornamented with cheerful villages and stately castles, Würtemberg lay spread before the eye of the beholder, in all the glory of the opening day. The unhappy Prince surveyed the scene with dejected looks. Nature had blessed him with a constancy of courage, and a heart which even grief and misery were unable to subdue; he possessed such control over his feelings that few were able to discern his inward suffering; and when calamity overtook him, then it was that the energies of his vigorous mind were most fertile in resources, and prompted him to immediate action.

In this truly heart-rending moment, when his last hope fell with the loss of his sole remaining castle, he concealed from his friends around him the painful conflict with which he was struggling. His feeling might be compared to the repentant son standing by the death-bed of a beloved mother, whose solicitude and anxiety for his welfare through life he had slighted, whose tender care of him in infancy he had forgotten, and the sacrifices she had imposed on herself to satisfy all his selfish wishes, even to the straitening of her own circumstances to meet the demands of his riotous living, he had treated with ingratitude, deeming them nothing more than his due. But now that her endearing eye no longer beholds him,--now that the ear is closed which was wont to listen to his wishes and complaints,--now that those hands no longer feel his last pressure,--then it is that repentance assails his heart,--then it is that his guilty conscience upbraids him with the bitter reproach of ingratitude and neglect of God's commandment,--to love, honour, and cherish father and mother.

Such was the anguish of self-condemnation which at this moment oppressed the breast of Ulerich of Würtemberg as he viewed his country, now to all appearance lost to him for ever. His noble nature, which he had too often abused in the blandishments of a brilliant court, and whose finer feelings had been deadened by the poisonous flattery of false friends, now upbraided him; not so much for being the author of his own personal misfortunes as for entailing on his country the distress attendant upon the occupation of it by his enemies.

Having stood for some time at the window, his mind harassed with these thoughts, he turned to his friends, who noticed in pleasing astonishment the calm expression of his countenance. They had dreaded his first burst of rage and violence, which they expected he would vent upon the treacherous conduct of his nobility. Instead of which, though he could not conceal the intensity of suffering he was struggling with, he was composed and resigned, and his features exhibited a mildness and resignation which they had scarcely ever seen before.

"Maxx," said he, "how have they acted towards the people of the country?"

"Like robbers," he answered: "they wantonly desolate the vineyards, cut down the fruit trees, and burn them at the guard houses; Sickingen's cavalry ride through the corn fields and tread down what they cannot consume; they ill treat the women, and extort money from the men. The people every where begin to murmur; and should the present drought continue, followed by a failing harvest, a time when the poor people will be called upon to pay the heavy expenses of the war which the league's administration will exact, misery and poverty will then be at its height."

"Oh, what villains!" cried the Duke, "they who boasted, with high sounding words, that they came to free Würtemberg of her tyrant, and to liberate her people from oppression now commit abominations even worse than Turks. But I vow that if God will assist me, and his holy saints be merciful to my soul, I will return to the wasted vallies of the Neckar and its vineless banks, with the scythe of vengeance, cut down their ranks like sheaves of corn, and, as a revengeful vine dresser, tread and crush them under foot. I will avenge myself of all the calamities they have brought on me and my country, so help me God!"

"Amen!" responded the knight of Lichtenstein. "But before you venture to the rescue of your country, you must first withdraw from it, for a season. No time is to be lost, if you would escape unmolested."

The Duke considered awhile, and then answered, "You are right, I will go to Mömpelgard, where I shall be able to make arrangements, and, I trust, collect men sufficient to venture to make a blow. Come here, thou faithful dog, thou wilt follow me into the misery of banishment. Thou knowest not what it is to break an oath or forfeit thy faith."

"Here stands another, who also knows nothing of treachery," said Schweinsberg, and approached the Duke. "I will accompany you to Mömpelgard, if you do not disdain my services."

The knight of Lichtenstein, animated by the same generous feeling, next said:. "Take me also with you, Duke! my feeble arm indeed is not worth much in the field, but my voice in council may still be heard."

Bertha's eyes lighted up more brilliantly than ever, as she beheld her lover, whose cheeks glowed with the ardour of youth, and whose looks bespoke the fire of his noble spirit.

"My Lord Duke," said he, "I proffered hand and arm in your service, when we met in the cavern, when I knew not who you were, and you did not refuse them. I aspire not to have a voice in council--but as you value a heart which beats faithful to you, an eye that will watch over you when you sleep, or an arm that will stand between you and your enemies, take me with you, and let me follow your fortune."

The noble feelings which had at first attached the young man to the "man without a name," now animated his breast, and the consideration of the Duke's misfortune, which he bore with such dignified magnanimity, added to the encouraging glance of his beloved, fed the flame of enthusiasm and devotion to the Duke's cause, and irresistibly threw him at his feet.

The old knight of Lichtenstein looked at his young guest with the joyous pride of a father; the Duke beheld him with emotion, and taking his hand, raised him from his knee and kissed his forehead.

"Where such hearts beat for us," said he, "we have still fortresses and walls to shelter us, and cannot bewail our poverty. You possess my love and esteem, Albert von Sturmfeder; you shall accompany me; I accept your faithful service with joy. Maxx Stumpf von Schweinsberg, I shall require your aid in more important business than to protect my body; I have a commission for you to execute in Hohentwiel and Switzerland. I cannot accept your company, good and faithful Lichtenstein. I honour you as a father, for your kindness to me has been such. You opened your door to me every night. I will repay it. When I return to my country, with God's help and will, your voice shall be the first in council."

The Duke's eye fell upon the fifer of Hardt, who stood aloof in humble retirement. "Come here, thou faithful man!" he called to him, and gave him his right hand, "you once were guilty of a great crime, but you have repented of it sincerely, and by faithful service regained my confidence."

"To attempt another's life is not so soon expiated," said the peasant, with downcast looks: "I am still in your grace's debt, but I will requite it when the time comes."

"Go to your home--such is my will--follow your occupations as heretofore. Perhaps you may be able to collect some faithful hearts in our cause by the time we return to our country. And you, lady! how can I reward your kindnesses? You deprived yourself many a night of rest, to open the door for me and shelter me against treachery! Do not blush so, as if you had some great sin to confess, this being the moment to act. Venerable father," said he, turning to the knight of Lichtenstein, "I appear before you as the intercessor of a couple of loving hearts. You will not disdain the son-in-law whom I propose to you?"

"I do not understand you, gracious Lord," said the knight, looking with astonishment at his daughter.

The Duke took Albert's hand, and led him to the old man. "This young man loves your daughter, and she is not indifferent to him,--what think you of making them a happy couple? But what means that frown of displeasure? Is he not high born, a gallant antagonist, the strength of whose arm I have already experienced, and now become my support in the hour of need?"

Bertha cast her eyes down, her face was suffused with blushes, she trembled for the reply of her father, who looked sternly at the young man. "Albert," said he, "I have had a high opinion of you since the first moment I saw you; it had been, perhaps, not so favourable, had I been aware of the object which brought you to my house."

The youth was about to make an answer, but the Duke interrupted him. "You forget that it was I who sent him to you with my seal and letter--he came not of his own accord. But what are you thinking of so long? I will adopt him as my son, and reward him with a property which will make you proud to call him your son-in-law."

"Do not trouble yourself further upon this point, my Lord Duke," said Albert, indignantly, when he noticed the indecision of the knight of Lichtenstein. "It shall never be said of me, that the heir of the Sturmfeders begged for a wife, and obtruded his importunity to gain the consent of a father against his free will. My name is too dear to me to resort to such means." He was about to leave the room in displeasure, but the old knight held him by the hand: "Hot-headed youth," he cried, "restrain your impetuosity? there, take her, she is yours, but--you must not think of leading her home, so long as an enemy's banner floats over the towers of Stuttgardt. Be faithful to the Duke, help him to return to his country, and if you continue true to his cause, the day that you enter the gates of the capital, when Würtemberg shall see her ensigns floating again over the pinnacles of her castles, my daughter from that moment shall be yours, and you shall then become my cherished son-in-law."

"And on that day," spoke the Duke, "the bride will blush more beautifully than ever, when the merry bells peal from the towers, and the marriage procession moves to the church. I will then approach the bridegroom, and demand the reward to which I claim a right. But now, my good friend, give her the bridal kiss, which is probably not the first, embrace her once more, and then you belong to me, until that happy day when we enter Stuttgardt. Let's drink, my friends, to the health of the happy couple."

A smile mingled with the tears of Bertha, which gleamed in her beautiful eyes. She filled the goblet to the brim, and having tasted the wine, a custom in those days done by the cup-bearers at courts, presented it first to the Duke, with a look so full of gratitude and lovely grace, that he thought Albert the happiest man in the world, and that many a one would not have hesitated to risk his life in order to gain a gem of her worth.

The men took each their goblet, waiting for a toast, which the Duke should give after his fashion. But Ulerich von Würtemberg, casting a long farewell look at his country, which he was about to quit, felt a tear start in his eye, which forced him to tear himself away from the painful view. "I now turn my back," said he, "upon objects which are dear to me, but, please God! I'll see them again in better days. Do not bewail my fate, but be of good cheer: as long as the Duke and his trusty friends are united, our good cause is not lost. 'Here's to good Würtemberg for ever!'"

FOOTNOTE TO CHAPTER XXIV.:

Footnote 1: If a crushed world should fall in upon him, the ruins would strike him undismayed.

CHAPTER XXV

In Swabia did thy princely father reign

Beloved, and all did glad allegiance yield;

And of the people, many now remain

Who fought beneath thy banners in the field.

Sure memory cannot be in Swabia dead.

Towards Swabia let us then our footsteps turn,

And as we the Black Forest's mazes tread,

Reviving hopes will in our bosoms burn.

L. Uhland.

So hot a summer as that of the year 1519, had scarcely ever been known in Würtemberg. The whole country had submitted to the power of the League, and its inhabitants now hoped their troubles were at an end. But the original intentions of its chiefs only began now to be fully developed, and it was evident that the mere reoccupation of Reutlingen was not the sole object for which they had coalesced. They were still to be indemnified for their expenses, and to be requited for their services. Some were for dividing Würtemberg equally among themselves, others proposed to sell it to Austria, whilst a third party insisted upon keeping it under the administration of Ulerich's children, subject to their own guardianship. They quarrelled about the possession of the country, to which none of them could found the slightest claims. Disunion and party spirit spread their baneful effects among them, now that they had satisfied their revenge in driving the legitimate lord from his dominions. The expenses of the war were to be met, and there was no one who could or would pay. The knights held this a favourable opportunity to declare themselves independent. Citizens and peasants were drained of their money by continual forced contributions, their fields were desolated and trodden under foot, and they saw no prospect of recovering their losses. Neither would the clergy contribute to the expenses of the war; so that the result of it was only dispute and violence. Many a heart felt how cruelly their legitimate prince had been persecuted, and bitterly repented having driven him into banishment, far from the land of his fathers. And when they compared his system of government with that of their present rulers, they found they had not bettered themselves by the change; on the contrary, they were much worse off than before. But they were too much under subjection to venture to publish their grievances.

The discontent of the people did not escape the government of the League. Their ears were not shut to "much strange and wicked talk," as we read in old official documents. They tried to gain adherents to their cause by rigorous measures. They spread lies concerning the Duke; one of which was, that he had cut a boy of noble blood in halves, of the name of Wilhelm von Janowitz. It made a great noise at the time, but when he was pointed out some time afterwards to a Swiss, as the man of whom the enemies of Ulerich had spread the report, he gave for answer, "He must indeed have been a good carpenter who put the boy so well together again." The priests were ordered to announce from the pulpit, that whoever spoke favourably of the Duke was to be put in prison, and those who supported or assisted him were to lose their eyes, and perhaps their heads.

Ulerich had many faithful friends among the country people, who secretly gave him intelligence how things were going on in Würtemberg. He remained in Mömpelgard with the men who had followed him in his misfortune, waiting a favourable moment to return to his country. He wrote to many Princes, imploring their assistance, but none would bestir themselves in his behalf. He petitioned also the Electors, assembled for the purpose of electing a new Emperor. The only aid they rendered him was to oblige the new Emperor to add an additional clause to his contract, favourable to Würtemberg and the Duke,--but he paid no attention to it. Though he felt himself thus deserted by all the world, he did not give way to despondency, but set all his energies at work to recover his lost country by the resources of his own mind. Many circumstances appeared to favour his project: the League, having satisfied themselves that no one would dare shelter the exile in the country, disbanded most of their troops, composed chiefly of lansquenet, retaining only weak garrisons in the towns and castles; and in Stuttgardt itself, the capital, there remained but few infantry under their banners.

These measures of the League, however, were the cause of creating a formidable enemy to themselves, in a quarter they did not suspect, but which very soon contributed essentially to produce a change in the Duke's favour. This enemy were the common foot soldiers, or the lansquenet. This body of men, collected together from all ends and corners of the empire, and composed of all nations, generally offered their services to those who paid them best. The cause for which they were to fight was perfectly indifferent to them. Being a licentious set, and difficult to be restrained even by severity of discipline, they indemnified themselves by robbery, murder, plunder, and forcibly exacting contributions, if they were not regularly paid. George von

Fronsberg had been the first to keep them in some measure in subordination, and by the renown of his name, by daily exercise, and unbending severity, succeeded in forming them into something like an army. He divided them into regular companies and brigades, appointed special officers to each, and taught them to move and fight in columns and masses. These men now shewed that they came from a good school, for when the League disbanded them they did not, as formerly, separate and spread over the country, seeking service individually, but confederating together, formed twelve companies, chose their own commanders from among themselves, and appointed their general in the person of a man who went by the name of *Long Peter*. Being exasperated against the League, and living upon plunder and forced contributions, they became the dread of the whole country. Anarchy had spread its baneful spirit throughout Würtemberg to such a degree, that no one was able to resist their depredations. The party of the League was enfeebled by continual disunion, and was too much employed with its own affairs to think of freeing the impoverished land of this formidable band. The knights, being at variance with each other, remained shut up in their castles, looking on with indifference at the state of affairs. The garrisons of the towns were weak, and not able to repel them by force. The citizens and peasantry, when they were not hard pressed by these marauders, treated them civilly, being equally averse to the government of the League, whom no one now favoured; it was even said they were not disinclined to reinstate the Duke, by the assistance of the same arms that had dethroned him.

On a fine morning of the month of August this body was assembled, and encamped in a meadow of a valley touching the boundary of Baden. Tall black firs and pines encompassed the spot on three sides, and formed part of the Black Forest, with the rivulet called the Würm running through it. Partly under the shade of the wood, partly stretched out among the bushes of the meadow, the little army was distributed about in different groups, taking their rest. At the distance of about two hundred paces were to be seen advanced posts of armed men on the look-out, whose shining lances and lighted matches inspired dread and awe to the by-passer. In the middle of the valley, under the shade of a large oak tree, sat five men, round an out-spread cloak, which served them for a table, where they were playing at a game of cards, called to this day lansquenet. These men were distinguished from the rest of their companions by a broad red scarf, hanging down over the shoulder and breast; but their dress had otherwise much the same ragged worn-out appearance with the others. Some of them wore helmets, others large felt hats, bound with iron, and all of them leather jerkins, of every possible shade and colour, which long service in rain, dust, and bivouacing had imparted to them. Upon a closer inspection, there were two things which particularly distinguished them from the rest of their comrades.

They had neither gun nor pike, which were the ordinary weapons of the lansquenet, but wore rapiers of uncommon length and breadth. They also carried in their hats and helmets, in fashion with the nobility and leaders of armies of those days, cock's tail feathers of various colours, assuming to themselves the rank of superiority.

These five men, particularly one who was seated with his back to the tree, appeared much interested in the game which they were playing. He wore a hat with a brim of the breadth of a good sized millstone, trimmed with dingy gold lace, and ornamented in front with a gilt portrait of Saint Peter, out of which sprang two enormous red cock's feathers. His language was a compound of French, Italian, and Hungarian, put together in such strange mixture, that he was scarcely intelligible to those to whom he addressed himself. No one knew what country gave him birth; but he commanded a certain respect among his comrades from the fact of his having served in most of the armies of Europe, and been in nearly all the campaigns of his day; and as he generally prefaced most of his phrases with oaths which he had picked up in the countries he had passed through, and which he pronounced after his own fashion, he thought to render himself thereby of more consequence among those over whom he had assumed the title of general. His beard was dressed in the Hungarian fashion, for being twisted up with pitch, it stuck out on both sides from under his nose a whole span's breadth in the air, much like two iron spikes.

"*Canto cacramento!*" cried this man, with a threatening bass voice, "the little knave is mine; I'll cut him with the king of spades!"

"It's mine, with your permission," cried his neighbour, "and the king into the bargain; there's the queen of spades!"

"Morbleu!" vociferated the other, in a rage; "do you want to take the trick from your commander, Captain Löffler? For shame, for shame! he is a rebel who dares do that. May my soul be punished, but you want to take the command away from me." The general, for such he was, frowned furiously, pushed his hat off his ears, and discovered a large red scar on his forehead, which heightened the savage appearance of his look.

"There is no military discipline at play," General Peter, "answered the other. You may order us captains to blockade a town, and raise contributions, but at play one man is as good as another."

"You are mutinous, a rebel against the authorities! Thunder and lightning! were it not against my honour, I would cut you into a hundred pieces;--but play on."

"There's an ace," said one. "Here's a quart," said another. "I cut with the ten," exclaimed a third. "And here's the knave,--who can take him?" said the fourth player.

"I can," cried the large man; "there's the king,--Morbleu! the trick is mine."

"Where did you get the king?" said a little thin man, with a cunning face, small searching eyes, and shrill voice, "didn't I see it at the bottom of the pack when you dealt. He has cheated! Long Peter has cheated, by all the saints!"

"Muckerle, captain of the eighth company! I advise you to hold your tongue," said the general; "*Bassa manelka!* I don't take a joke,--the mouse should not play with the lion."

"And I say it again,--where did you get the king? I'll prove you false before the pope and the king of France, thou foul player."

"Muckerle," replied the general, drawing his sword deliberately out of its scabbard, "pray another Ave Maria and a Gratias, for as soon as the game is over you are a dead man."

The other three men were roused from a state of indifference at these angry words. They sided with the little captain, and gave the general to understand clearly that they thought he was capable of the imputed meanness. He, however, looked big, and full of importance, and swore he had not cheated. "If the holy Peter, my gracious patron, who I carry on my hat, could speak, he would bear me witness, as true as I am a Christian lansquenet, that I have not played false!"

"He played fair," said a strange voice, which appeared to issue from the tree. The men crossed themselves to defend them from an evil spirit, the gallant general even turned pale, and let drop his cards; when a peasant stept forward from behind the tree, armed with a dagger, and having a guitar slung over his shoulder with a leathern strap. He beheld the group with an undaunted eye, and said, "That gentleman did not cheat; I saw all the cards that were dealt to him."

"Ah! you are a fine fellow," said the general, much pleased; "as I am an honest lansquenet, what you say is all right."

"But how is this?" said the little captain, with a sharp look, "how did this peasant get here without being announced by the piquet? He is a spy, and deserves to be hung."

"Don't be astonished, Muckerle, he is no spy; come and sit down by me, my friend, you are a musician, I see, by your instrument hanging over your shoulder, like a Spaniard going to serenade his love."

"Yes, sir! I am a poor musician; your guard allowed me to pass when I came through the wood. I saw you playing, and I ventured to look on."

The commanders of this free corps not being accustomed to hear themselves addressed in such polite terms, took a liking to the peasant, and invited him courteously to seat himself among them; for they had learned in the military service of foreign countries that kings and princes often went about in the guise of minstrels.

The general filled a cup of wine out of a pewter bottle, offered it to the little captain, and said, with a good-natured smile, "Muckerle, what I drink shall be my death, if I don't forget everything that has passed between us! an end to strife and quarrel. We won't play any more, gentlemen: I love a song and the sound of the guitar--what say you to some music?"

The men agreed, and threw the cards aside. The peasant tuned his instrument, and asked what he should sing.

"Give us a song upon card-playing!" cried one of the party.

The musician considered awhile, and sung the following upon the game of lansquenet, which they had just been playing.

"Cinque, quatre, and ace

Bring many a man to disgrace;

Quatre, and cinque, and tré

Make many to cry well-a-day;

An ace, a seize, and a deuce

Make many an empty house;

A quatre, a trois, and cinque

Cause many pure water to drink;

A cinque, a trois, and quatre

Make parents' and children's eyes water;

From cinque, and quatre, and seize,

Miss Catherine and Miss Elize

Must long unmarried remain,

Unless from your play you refrain."

Long Peter and his associates praised his singing, and reached him the flask with their thanks. "May God bless you!" said the singer, as he returned the bottle; "I wish you luck in your campaign. If I don't mistake, you are the commanders of the League, and are on your march to the enemy. May I ask who you are going against?"

The men looked and smiled at each other, but the general answered him: "you are quite in the wrong. We did, indeed, serve the League formerly, but we are now free and our own masters, ready to assist any one who wants us."

"This will be a good year for the Swiss, for it is said the Duke will return to his country with their assistance," said the peasant.

"May the Swiss be hunted by wolves," said the general, "for having treated him so ill! The good Duke set all his hopes upon them, and, *diavolo maledetto*! did they not desert him in Blaubeuren?"

"Yes, it was too bad," said Captain Muckerle; "but when one looks at the circumstance in its proper light, it served him half right, because he should have known them better. May the devil take them all!"

"They were the Duke's last resource," replied the musician; "but if he had trusted to such men as you, the League would still be at Ulm."

"You have spoken a true word there, my hearty friend!" said the captain. "He ought to have preferred the lansquenets before those Swiss dogs. And if he trusts to them now, I know what will happen. I say it again: he should take lansquenets. Is it not so, Magdeburger?"

"That's my opinion also," said the Magdeburger: "no other than lansquenets can seat the Duke upon his chair again. The Swiss only know how to use their long halberds; that's all their art. But you ought to see us load our guns, how we lay them in the fork, and fire them with a match. No one can come near us in that manœuvre. The Swiss take half an hour to fire their guns, but we only half of a quarter."

"With all respect, gentlemen of this noble corps," said the peasant, raising his cap respectfully, "the Duke should certainly have thrown himself upon your bounty. But the League rewarded you too well for the poor Duke to be able to crave your assistance."

"Rewarded, did you say?" cried the captain of the fifth company, and laughed; "yes, those Swabian dogs would have melted gold out of lead if they could! But I say they paid us ill, and if his grace the Duke will take me, my services are at his command."

"You are right, Staberl," said the general, and stroked his beard. "*Morbleu!* the cat likes to have his back stroked:--if the Duke pays well, the whole corps will join him."

"Well, you shall soon see that," said the peasant, with a cunning smile; "have you had an answer to your message to the Duke?"

The general's whole countenance became as red as fire at this question. "*Mordelement!* Who are you, child of man, who knows my secret? Who told you I had sent to the Duke?"

"Did you, Peter, send to him? What secret have you between each other that we should not know? Tell us immediately," said the Magdeburger.

"Well, I thought it was my duty to think for you all again, as I always have done, and sent a man to the Duke in our name, and with our compliments, to know if he required our services? Our terms were, half a broad piece a man per month, and for us generals and captains a gold florin, with four measures of old wine."

"Those are no bad terms: a gold florin a month! none of us will object to them. Have you had an answer from the Duke?" said the Magdeburger.

"Not yet," said the general. "But, *bassa manelka!* tell me, how do you come to know my secret, peasant, or I'll cut off your ear, and pin it to my hat? Tell me immediately, or off it comes."

"Long Peter," cried the little captain Muckerle, "let him go in peace, for God's sake! he is a resolute man, and possesses the art of witchcraft. I recollect his face as well as if it was but to-day, when we had orders to arrest him in Ulm, and were sent to look for him at the stable of Herrn von Kraft, the clerk of the council, where he resided. He was a spy, and was able to make himself smaller and smaller, not bigger than a sparrow, and flew away from us."

"What!" cried the gallant general, and edged away from the peasant; "is this the man? Why did not the magistrates of Ulm order all the sparrows to be shot, because a Würtemberger spy had turned himself into one?"

"That's him," whispered Muckerle; "that's the fifer of Hardt; I knew him as soon as I saw him."

The general and his companions did not recover their astonishment for some time. They beheld the man of whom many wonderful stories had been related with mingled curiosity and apprehension. Hans was clever enough, however, to understand what they whispered to each other, without the appearance of remarking the state of surprise he had created among them. At length, Long Peter, the official organ of the rest, took heart, twisted his whiskers, and, taking off his enormous hat, thus addressed the fifer of Hardt: "Pardon us, worthy companion, and highly respected fifer of Hardt, that we have treated you with so little ceremony; but how could we know who it was we had among us? be many times welcome; I have long wished to see so renowned a man as the fifer of Hardt, who had the power of flying away from Ulm like a sparrow in the middle of the day."

"Let's have done with those old stories," interrupted the fifer, hastily. "I heard this day from the Duke, who desired me to find you out, to know if you were still inclined to join him upon the terms he has proposed."

"*Canto cacramento!* he is a good man! a gold ducat a month and four measures of wine daily! Long may he live!" cried the general.

"When will he come?" asked captain Löffler. "Where shall we meet him?"

"This very day, if no ill luck attends him. He was to advance upon Heimsheim this morning, where the garrison is weak, and, when he has taken it, he will come on this way."

"Look! there rides a man in armour, to all appearance a knight!" The men looked towards the end of the valley, and remarked a helmet and armour shining in the sun, with a horse occasionally visible. The fifer of Hardt jumped up and climbed the oak, whence he could overlook the valley with greater ease. The horseman was too distant from him to be able to recognise his features, but he thought he knew the scarf which he wore, and that it was the person he had been expecting to appear.

"What do you see?" said the men; "is it one riding by chance through the wood, or do you think he comes from the Duke?"

"That's him with the white and blue scarf," said the fifer; "that's his long hair, and his seat on horseback. Oh, precious youth, welcome back to Würtemberg! He observes your advanced post, and rides towards it; only look how the fellows present their lances and spread out their legs!"

"Yes, yes, the lansquenet knows the arts of war; no one dare pass the spot where the commanders are, without knowing his business," said the general.

"Stop! they are calling to him; he speaks to them; they point this way; he comes!" cried the fifer, who came down from the tree with a joyful countenance.

"*Diavolo maledetto! bassam terendete!* They won't let him ride alone, I hope? Ah! I see one of them has hold of his bridle 1 How? It is really a knight that comes!

"A nobleman as good as any in the empire," answered the fifer; "the friend and favourite of the Duke." Upon hearing this they all stood up, for, though they fancied themselves men of importance and rank, they were aware of their being only lansquenets, and bound to pay proper respect to their superiors. The general seated himself again, with an air of gravity, at the foot of the oak--stroked his beard to make it shine--arranged his hat with the cock's feathers properly--supported his hand on his enormous sword-- and in this manner awaited the arrival of the stranger.